Puffin Plus
WARGAMES

'Sir,' Colonel Cowley said, 'we have a radar tracking of eight inboard Soviet ICBMs already over the pole ... Estimated impact ... twelve ... make that eleven minutes. Confirmed target area: western United States.'

The graphics on the computer screens deep in the control centre showed the awful truth: that the long-expected, long-feared moment had arrived at last when the nation was to be blitzed by foreign missiles.

Or was it? Up in the city of Seattle, seventeen-year-old David Lightman, computer freak and ace games player, was getting some pretty amazing results on his computer screen as he typed rapidly into the terminal. Could it be that he had typed himself right into the nation's sophisticated defence systems – and set off a *real* war alert?

Wargames is a tense computer-age thriller, often funny but more often quite alarming in its portrayal of the havoc that one clever boy can cause.

David Bischoff

WARGAMES

Based on the original screenplay
written by Lawrence Lasker and Walter F. Parkes

Puffin Books

Puffin Books, Penguin Books Ltd, Harmondsworth, Middlesex, England
Penguin Books, 40 West 23rd Street, New York, New York 10010, USA
Penguin Books Australia Ltd, Ringwood, Victoria, Australia
Penguin Books Canada Ltd, 2801 John Street, Markham, Ontario, Canada L3R 1B4
Penguin Books (NZ) Ltd, 182–190 Wairau Road, Auckland 10, New Zealand

First published in the USA by Dell Publishing Co., Inc., 1983
Published in Great Britain in Penguin Books 1983
This adapted edition published simultaneously in Puffin Books

Made and printed in Great Britain by
Cox & Wyman Ltd, Reading
Filmset in Monophoto Photina by Northumberland Press Ltd, Gateshead

To Kate Ennis,
most affectionately

Prologue

Snow.

The flakes came thick as TV static, muffling the growls of the Air Force van's engines as the vehicle carried the two officers toward their deadly night duty.

'Crummy day to guard the nation, huh?' Lieutenant Ulmer said. Ulmer's hands held the steering wheel with the casual ease of the practiced snow driver, but his eyes stayed glued to the icy North Dakota road. Numberless windblown flakes fluttered through the arcs of the van's headlights, cutting visibility to near zero.

Ulmer's companion grunted. 'Yeah, the sky's taken a dump on the Red River Valley, all right. I used to serve in Alaska, though, so I've seen worse.'

Nonetheless, Captain Jerry Hallorhan huddled tighter in his parka, glaring at the faulty heater. These stupid Air Force vans, he thought. They can keep a half-dozen Blue Angels in precision flight, but they can't heat a crummy four-wheeler.

'Maybe we'll get a medal just for getting there,' Ulmer suggested, shifting down to second for a slight upward grade.

'Cripes, Lieutenant,' Hallorhan said, sinking lower in his seat, 'if a guy on button jockey duty does somethin' to get a medal for, chances are there ain't gonna be no one around to pin it on his irradiated chest!'

Hallorhan barked a coarse laugh, then honked his nose into his handkerchief.

It figured. Cold coming on. His sinuses were allergic to snow, no question. When he had enough seniority, he'd make damn sure he was located in someplace like Arizona, warmer. Gladys would like that. The kids too. His nose would *love* it.

Hallorhan wiped his nose and sighed. His breath misted.

'You were telling me about that hippie girl friend you used to have, Sheila,' Steve Ulmer said as he put the column shift back into third. 'Sounds like quite a lady.'

Hallorhan smiled to himself. 'Oh, yes. The one back near Andrews Air Force Base. Those were the days, all right. Protests, and parties, acid rock, and free love. Sheila was right there with them, a real radical. Boy, she'd have a fit if she knew what I was doing *now*! When she wasn't off sucking in tear gas on Route One at the University of Maryland, she was draggin' me to see some Godard film, or *Hiroshima Mon Amour*. We saw *Dr Strangelove* musta been three times!'

'Anti-nuke, huh,' Ulmer said, somberly.

'Yeah, but it was all worth it!' Hallorhan said, almost defensively. 'One tripped-out lady, Sheila! Really into Eastern mysticism, you know? And causes ...! We had some fine times, I tell you! She did some of the weirdest things. Like, she had this *forest* of plants and –'

Ulmer peered through the dimness ahead. 'Center's coming up,' he said.

'About time!' Hallorhan fumbled with the satchel to his side, locked to his left wrist. 'My momma used to put gloves on me this way. They musta talked to her before they stuck me on this gig!'

'Right.' Ulmer laughed as he wedged the van into a parking slot by the guard gate.

'Geronimo!' cried Hallorhan, bracing himself for the chill. He pushed the door open and stepped into a pile of frosty white stuff. The wind struck him hard and pushed him against the van's fender. He cursed and looked up. Flakes were driven into his eyes. He pulled his hood up. Before them a building that looked like a farm house rose from snowdrifts. Lieutenant Ulmer was already bashing his way through the weather.

'Friggin' New Air Force,' Hallorhan muttered, driving his burly form after his junior officer.

Ulmer made it to the door first and held it open for the captain. Hallorhan stepped into the warmth, immediately kicking off his snow-clogged boots and slipping off his parka, revealing a bright blue jumpsuit with 321ST MISSILE WING emblazoned on the back. A bright red ascot snuggled around his neck.

'Sure feels a hell of a lot better in here, huh?' the captain said, fooling with the lock on his satchel.

'Sure does,' agreed Ulmer. He grinned as Hallorhan finally opened the lock and pulled a red folder out of the satchel. Hallorhan approached a bulletproof glass and slipped the folder to the expressionless guard.

The guard flipped open the folder, studied the two photo IDs enclosed, then peered blankly up at the new arrivals. He picked up a phone and punched out a number.

'Replacement team's here, sir,' he said. A smile crept over his face. 'Right.' He hung up the phone. 'Come on through.

Another twenty minutes and we were going to start looking for you.'

'Yeah,' Hallorhan said. 'Gotta warn ya, kid . . .' he said to Ulmer, ' 'round Minuteman III missile launch control centers, you go AWOL, you get *nuked*!'

The guard shook his head at the grim joke, then leaned over and hit a button. A buzz sounded, unlocking the door. The two officers pushed through into the secure area.

The guard checked out their faces again, then returned the folder. He pulled out a pair of holstered service pistols and flopped them in front of the missilemen.

Ulmer buckled his on. 'See you tomorrow,' he said to the guard.

Their footsteps echoed as they pounded down a corridor toward an elevator door. Hallorhan buckled on his holster.

A young sentry clutching an M-16 snapped to attention. The officers ignored him. Lieutenant Ulmer hit the button, then allowed his superior to step into the elevator first.

'So anyway,' Hallorhan said, eager to continue his story. 'I used to hear Sheila chanting all night long, "ah mahney pod me ohm, ah mahney pod me ohm." '

'Over the *plants?*' Ulmer was incredulous.

'Yeah! She'd hold her hands over the seeds and chant by the hour. Grew the most beautiful plants you ever saw. She was a real strange lady!'

The elevator door parted, revealing the base's underground launch level. Enough concrete and steel here to build a city, Hallorhan thought. A five-megaton warhead would be like a cherry bomb to this baby, yes sir!

As Hallorhan stepped out of the elevator ahead of Ulmer, an alarm began to wail.

Hallorhan stepped briskly to the blast door. After punching a code into a keyboard, he spoke into an intercom.

'This is Captain Hallorhan. Ready to authenticate.' He took a breath. 'Lima, Oscar, November, Lima, Whiskey, Golf.' He winked at Ulmer.

The alarm stopped. Good. Hallorhan's head was ringing. It always did. *Must be the pitch*, he figured.

Hidden motors whirred. Locking pins withdrew. The two men pushed the door open and passed through into another corridor, trapising up to a second blast door.

'Avon calling,' Hallorhan said.

The door opened for them.

They casually saluted the team they were replacing.

The missile commander, Captain Ed Flanders, stood up from his chair by the entrance controls, rubbing his stomach and stretching lazily. 'We were worried about you guys.' He glanced over to his deputy, Lieutenant Morgan, who sat by one of the launch controls, penning readings onto a form clamped by a clipboard. 'The roads must be –'

'What roads?' Hallorhan said sardonically.

Their overnight home was a capsule ten feet by twenty feet, a technophobe's nightmare. Lights blipped. Fans hummed. The faint aroma of electricity mingled with a hint of unwashed socks and a trace of strong coffee. The place was crammed with panels of high-frequency transmitters, circuit breakers, air purification and backup systems. A high-speed teleprinter with a direct line to Strategic Air Command head-quarters sat mute in a corner. A refrigerator hummed in another corner. A small and very unprivate latrine huddled whitely in yet another. Each of the two launch consoles possessed a computer terminal and large annunciator panels

11

displaying the status of each of the ten missiles controlled by this capsule.

Mounted on the capsule wall was a bright red strongbox, secured by two locks.

Captain Flanders peered closer at Hallorhan, then pointed disbelievingly at his face. 'What is *that*?'

Jerry blinked. 'That? That's a mustache,' he said indignantly.

'New image!' said Ulmer.

The deputy put the clipboard down and headed for the open door.

'Well, gentlemen,' said Captain Flanders, following suit. 'Have a good one!'

As Hallorhan closed the blast door behind the departing team, Ulmer unstrapped his holster, hung it on a hook, and settled uneasily into the red chair of his console. The kid was fresh, thought Hallorhan as he walked over to a mirror. But he'd get broken in real quick. Already the fellow was running through a checklist of the console functions.

Hallorhan stared at his reflection. Gladys had given him hell about the mustache too. She said that it tickled when they kissed. Not that they kissed that often these days.

Ulmer was already at work. 'Number three is still off alert, sir. Other than that all nine birds are clean and green with no warnings at this time.'

Hallorhan fingered his mustache. '*I* like it,' he said.

'So this crazy lady ...' Ulmer said as his hands floated over a series of buttons. 'She was really anti-war, right?' A row of lights activated. A buzzer sounded. Ulmer cleared the buzzer by quickly pushing a second relay.

Hallorhan went over and checked out the refrigerator.

'Anti-war? Sheila was such a pacifist, she would have made Gandhi look like Genghis Khan by comparison.'

Milk for coffee. Some cellophane-wrapped Hostess Sno Balls. A carton of takeout Chinese that had been sitting there for a week. Some fruit. The nerve wracking drive had given Hallorhan the munchies. He selected an apple and turned to watch what his deputy was up to.

He chomped noisily. Sour. It figured.

A red light on a panel failed to respond to the release button. Lieutenant Ulmer stiffened. 'Sir, red light.'

Hallorhan walked forward to get a better view. 'What on?'

Ulmer's eyes stayed fixed on the console, as if he'd seen a ghost. 'Number eight, warhead alarm,' he said flatly.

Hallorhan chuckled. 'Just give it a thump with your finger.'

Clearly relieved, Ulmer tapped the light. It blinked off immediately.

As Ulmer went on with his checklist, Hallorhan strode over to his own console twelve feet from the lieutenant's, sat down, made a cursory survey of the equipment, then propped his feet up on the console and began daydreaming about Sheila as he clipped his fingernails.

Hallorhan thumbed a page of his paperback detective novel. This guy Spenser was great, he thought. He'd have to check out the other books by Robert B. Parker. The detective was getting the crap beaten out of him when a voice began to warble over the loudspeaker.

'Skybird, this is Dropkick with a Blue Dash Alpha message in two parts. Break, break.'

The novel slapped onto the floor as Hallorhan's training

propelled him into instant action. He stood and grabbed the format book from its shelf above the console. He quickly flipped through it. Where the hell was it ... Ah. He found a blue plastic page marked BLUE DASH ALPHA/WOPR. He fumbled for the felt marker.

This was weird, Hallorhan thought. 'Stand by to copy message,' he ordered.

Ulmer was on the ball. 'Standing by,' he said, clutching his own book of instructions.

The voice resumed. 'Blue Dash Alpha ... Blue Dash Alpha Romeo, Oscar, November, Charlie, Tango, Tango, Lima.'

Quickly Hallorhan copied the code into the spaces provided in the format book.

'Authentication,' the voice continued. 'Delta, Lima, Gold, two, two, four, zero, niner, Tango, Victor, X ray.'

Again his training seemed to power him automatically. He stepped to the strongbox. Ulmer was already there.

Hallorhan attacked his combination lock. He had it off a mere second before Ulmer had his off. Hallorhan pushed the lid up. Both men removed their brass keys and plastic card authenticator marked BLUE-A.

Hurrying back to his console, Hallorhan nervously ripped the seal off his authenticator. His fingers were trembling. He took a deep, long breath, then compared the letters on the authenticator card with those he had just copied down.

They matched!

Displayed on the computer screen was another series of letters. Hallorhan examined them carefully.

Identical!

'Oh, wow!' said Ulmer.

Hallorhan couldn't tear his eyes from the screen.

'Easy now.' He swallowed, calming himself. 'Run a confirmation. Some idiot must have his wires crossed.'

Carefully, Hallorhan tapped the query into his computer terminal. Twelve feet away, Lieutenant Steve Ulmer was doing the same.

'Come on, baby,' Hallorhan said through gritted teeth. 'Show us it's *wrong*!'

Letters paraded silently across his screen.

LAUNCH ORDER CONFIRMED.

TARGET SELECTION COMPLETE.

ENABLE MISSILES.

LAUNCH TIME MINUS 60 SECONDS.

BEGIN COUNTDOWN.

Hallorhan stared long seconds at the readout. The voice from the loudspeaker interrupted his reverie.

'T-sixty, T-fifty-nine, T-fifty-eight . . .'

Ulmer's voice was a monotone: 'Oh, God! It's real!'

Hallorhan licked his lips. 'All right. Let's do it.' His training dragged those words out of him. Eighteen years in the Air Force tugged his body down into the chair; he pulled the seat belt up around his stomach and buckled it. All the rest of him was stunned.

They tell you how to do this, they tell you that it might have to be done, but they don't tell you how you're supposed to feel when those orders stream into your capsule.

Hallorhan took the key he'd grabbed from the red box and inserted it into a slot marked OFF, SET, LAUNCH.

Still on automatic, Hallorhan said, 'Insert lock codes.'

Ulmer played at the keyboard, setting the codes. His voice hung on to its monotone. 'Stand by . . . unlock codes inserted.'

Somewhere in the back of Captain Jerry Hallorhan's mind, past the training, past the surprise, past everything, a small voice seemed to be talking to him.

'Uh,' he said, his voice faltering. 'Insert launch key.'

'Roger. Launch key inserted.'

A memory bloomed. Sheila again. Sheila in one of her diatribes on nuclear war.

'Okay ...' Jerry said, staring ahead, his heart pounding, his mouth drying out. 'On my mark. Rotate launch key to "set".'

He twisted his key, and knew that Ulmer had turned his simultaneously.

'Roger,' Ulmer confirmed. 'At "set".'

In Jerry Hallorhan's memory, he heard Sheila speak: *The problem is that the concept is too big for little military minds to encompass. We're talking about weapons that are going to wipe out millions upon millions of human lives, just because of different ideologies. We're talking obliterated flesh and blood and possibility and hope and love. We're talking about the destruction of every*thing *that matters ... maybe forever. Imagine it, Jerry. Imagine it!*

Lieutenant Ulmer said, 'Sir?'

'Uh ...' Jerry said, starting. 'Enable missiles.'

Lieutenant Ulmer flipped the hubs off a series of protected switches. His face a study in concentration, he began the enabling procedure, flipping the toggles with practiced precision. 'Number one enabled ... number two enabled,' he droned. 'Number three enabled.'

Ten missiles would rocket out of their silos, punching through the blizzard outside, trailing hellfire tails, arcing through the stratosphere carrying their nuclear payloads. Over half would get shot out of the sky, but the rest would probably find their strategic targets, exploding over Russia, throwing up their familiar mushroom clouds.

'Number six enabled.'

Jerry could suddenly almost see the flesh being ripped from bone by the blasts.

'Wait a minute,' he said. 'I want to get this straight with somebody on the blasted phone.' He pulled up the receiver. A loud wail ripped into his ears. *Oh, no, that's what they said would happen if . . .*

He slammed the phone back into its cradle.

'All missiles are enabled,' Ulmer reported.

'Get me wing command post on *your* phone,' Hallorhan ordered, desperation creeping into his voice.

As though grabbing for hope himself, Ulmer picked up his phone. The wail was like a banshee's scream. Ulmer turned to Hallorhan, a hopeless questioning in his eyes.

Hallorhan grasped for another way out. 'SAC! Try SAC headquarters on the HF.'

'But Captain, this *isn't* the procedure.'

'Forget the procedure,' Hallorhan almost yelled. 'I want to get somebody on the stupid phone before I *kill* twenty million people!'

In his head he could hear Sheila talking again: *Have you ever seen radiation burns, Jerry? Have you seen what fallout will do to people?*

Ulmer desperately snatched up a headset, stuck one earpiece to his head. He stepped to a military transmitter and twisted at the channel selector, listening intently.

He sighed. 'Nothing.' A haunted look invaded his eyes. 'They've probably been . . . vaporized.'

Hallorhan sucked in a breath, let it go quickly. Gladys was

out there. And his kids. 'All right. On my mark. Rotate launch keys to launch.'

You're a good man, Captain Hallorhan, they had said. You've got what, ten years to go till voluntary retirement? Fine record. Yes, we think you fit the bill. We hope you realize this sort of duty is the highest honor bestowed upon an officer ... but it's also a grave responsibility.

Ulmer said, 'Roger. Ready to go to launch.'

You're going to have the future of the U.S. of A. at your fingertips, Captain Hallorhan, they had said. Your country is counting on you ...

'T-thirteen, T-twelve.'

The automatic countdown began through the speaker. Hallorhan joined in.

'T-eleven, T-ten ... T-ten.'

Sheila's words flooded his mind again: *But Jerry, you're not a machine, you're a human being. That's why I care for you! Don't let those idiots brainwash you!*

The words wouldn't come out of Hallorhan's mouth. They seemed stuck in his throat.

Ulmer turned to his commander, a look of alarm on his face. '... *Sir!* We have orders!'

Hallorhan did not respond. He looked at the lieutenant. Ulmer whipped out his .38 automatic and pointed it at his superior.

'Put ... put your hand on the key, sir,' Ulmer demanded, a note of apology in his voice.

'... T-six, T-five, T-four,' the loudspeaker announced.

Looking away, Hallorhan shook his head.

'I'm sorry.'

The countdown appeared in letters on the monitor.

'... T-three, T-two, T-one, *launch*,' said the voice.

Sheila's voice seemed more distant now, but still clear. *Make an ethical, no, a* moral *decision for once in your life, Jerry Hallorhan. Do something that matters!*

Ulmer was desperate. His voice was thin and shrill. 'Sir ... we are at launch! *Turn the key!*'

Jerry sat, suddenly calm and accepting, a vivid peace sweeping through him.

He turned to Lieutenant Ulmer and said, 'I can't.'

An earsplitting shriek filled the tiny capsule as Missile Commander Jerry Hallorhan waited silently for whatever came next.

Chapter One

The world ended not with a bang, nor even with a whimper, but in total silence.

Mushroom clouds sprouted from the green and brown surface of the planet Earth. Cracks began to zigzag through North and South America. Smoke issued forth in ragged plumes.

David Lightman said, 'What the hell?'

He put down his joystick, leaned over, and thumbed the volume of the ancient Sylvania nineteen-inch color TV. This produced higher static hum, background noise, but nothing else. On the screen the image of Earth crumbled, and bright crimson letters proclaimed:

FINIS

David Lightman leaned back in his chair and slapped his forehead. 'The subroutine for the final explosion!'

He'd completely forgotten the stupid thing! He laughed. Everything else he'd worked out for his program Planet Wreckers had been perfect! It was almost as good as Atari's Star Raiders cartridge. It had better graphics, better sound.

The seventeen-year-old boy turned off the switch of his battered Altair terminal, then clicked off his operating disc drive, which ground to a halt. Sheesh, he could use some new drives. But he wouldn't trade in the Altair for anything. Along with the extra memory-storage units and peripheral devices he'd rigged together, this stuff was state-of-the-art mad hacker material, stuck together with chewing gum and more than a little ingenuity.

Of course, if some IBM equipment fell into his lap, he wouldn't throw it away. But what he had suited his purposes just fine right now, thank you. True, it looked like an electronics graveyard set up in his bedroom, but it was *his*.

David sighed. He turned off the secondhand disk drive, waited for the busy light to fade, then switched on the Altair.

READY, the screen said presently.

David scratched his stomach through his Ozzy Osbourne T-shirt and considered. Everything else about the program was apparently fine. The cross hairs for the marauding aliens was great, the defending Earth ships were sheer dynamite, and the final cataclysm of Earth's destruction, signaling victory for the player, was truly gonzo. He wouldn't have to type out the whole thing.

Okay, now.

He typed in DOS – disk operating system. There was only a short pause, after which he was rewarded with a readout containing all the sections of the Planet Wreckers program.

There it was. He'd forgotten the name he had assigned it.

KERSMASH

It took up 005 sectors on the old Elephant disk. Hmmm. If he could link that up with the graphics in just the right way ...

He called up Basic again, then ordered: LIST 'D: KER-SMASH.'

Almost immediately the lines of the program section appeared on his screen, neatly numbered. He knew some machine language, but found that Basic was just as good for this particular program.

He turned on the IBM I machine beside him that he had to use as a printer, and typed: PRINT.

The typewriter began doing just that, with painful slowness. If only he had a decent printer ... even a dot matrix would do. But his mother's old IBM had to suffice, what with the nickel-and-dime life David Lightman led with his paltry allowance and the occasional off job.

'David!' called his father from downstairs. The old man never bothered to come up and knock on the door. He just yelled from the bottom of the steps. 'David! Dinner's ready!'

David sighed and went to the door. 'Gimme a minute, okay?'

'You eat it now, or you don't eat.'

'Sheesh!' When Mom fixed dinner, his father could give a damn when he showed up. But when Mom was out doing real estate and the old man whipped up chow, attendance was mandatory, even though Harold Lightman knew about as much about cooking as he did about quantum mechanics.

'I'll be right down. I gotta wash my hands!'

David went back to the printer.

Chunka-chunka-chunk said the IBM, its little ball plopping the letters and numbers neatly onto the back of a real estate flyer from a pack his mom had given him.

'Shake a leg, huh?' he said, impatiently tapping on the machine's green housing, gazing absently around his bedroom. Cripes, what a mess. Clothes were strewn on the floor and bed. If Mom ever got a look at the place, she'd have a fit. Good thing he kept his room locked. It was fine with his father, too, who seemed to consider the room a dungeon where the slavering brain-damaged genetic monster of the family was chained away from the sight of respectable folk.

'*David!* I'm getting very angry!'

'Okay, okay!'

The element typed out the last of the program section. David grabbed a thick notebook, a Bic pen, yanked the paper from the platen, and virtually galloped down the stairs.

He sat at the dining room table, placing his stuff to one side of his plate. His father, who reminded him of a younger version of Tom Bosley in *Happy Days*, stood at the stove. When he turned around, David saw that he was wearing an apron. Sheesh, how typical!

'Doing your homework?' Harold Lightman asked.

'Did it already,' David answered, spreading his stuff out beside the neatly set table.

'I want to see some better grades this semester, David!'

David chuckled to himself as he glanced at the printout. 'Yeah. Yeah, I think I can promise you that.'

'Good.' Stirring something in a pot, Mr Lightman walked to the table. He set the pot down on a hot pad.

David stared at the steaming contents incredulously. 'Beans and franks? I had to come running for beans and franks?'

Mr Lightman adjusted his rimless glasses, a hurt expression crossing his rounded features. 'My special concoction. There are braised onions and peppers in there, a dash of spice, Worcestershire sauce, bacon ... And I found some lettuce and tomato ...' He gestured at the bowl of torn vegetables to one side of the table. 'Well, you know your mother's very busy these days.'

'Yeah.' David spooned a pile of the dun-colored glop onto his plate.

Mr Lightman sat down and began eating, frowning all the while.

Let me see, David thought. *Did I leave myself enough numbers here. If I use a GOTO subroutine right here, I could* . . .

'You know, it would be very pleasant to have a decent conversation with you for once at the dinner table, David, instead of having you pore over that gobbledygook computer stuff of yours, or reading a science fiction book or doing something else obnoxious.'

'Dad, this is important to me,' David said wearily.

'Oh.' His father poured some Thousand Island dressing on his salad. 'What are you working on today?'

'Finishing up a program for a game.'

'Really.'

'Yeah. Maybe I can sell it, make some money.'

'Well, then there are practical uses. What kind of game?'

'Top secret, Dad. Maybe I'll show it to you when I'm finished.'

'Why not now?'

'You don't understand. It's not perfect yet. And then I gotta copyright it.'

'If you get some money, you might think of buying a new suit, David. And come to think of it, you might want to wear that suit more often to church. Pastor Clinton has been asking about you.'

'Worried about the state of my soul, huh?'

'He likes you, David.'

'Dad, he just wants to chalk me up in his Converted

Heathen tally, so he'll get Brownie points from Jesus. It's all a game to him.'

'Doesn't sound much different than you.'

'Huh?'

'You play games . . . these computer games . . . all the time.'

'Everything's a game, Dad.'

'And you have to learn how to win, eh?'

'Uh uh. You have to learn how to *make* the games.'

His father shook his head wearily, giving up. David went back to the program. His pop wasn't a bad sort, really, but his head was out in the ozone. Faulty programming. Yeah. David could imagine it.

```
10 REM HAROLD LIGHTMAN
20 PRINT 'THE LIFE OF MR NOBODY'
30 IF GOOD THEN GOTO HEAVEN
40 IF BAD THEN GOTO HELL
```

After scribbling down a few key 'sound' lines for the program, he set aside the notebook and began to hurry through his meal so he could hop upstairs and try them out.

Harold Lightman patted his lips with a paper napkin and set it down. 'David, the church youth fellowship meets tonight. I thought, since your mother's not here, you and I might go.'

'No thanks, Dad.'

With an exasperated shake of the head, his father left the table, carrying his plate with him. A clatter of plate in the sink issued from the kitchen. Harold Lightman barreled out, face red, flustered. 'You'd go out if I was taking you to your stupid video arcades, or to see an R-rated film, or to watch a punk rock band, wouldn't you!'

'Dad, please! It's called New Wave now.'

'I don't care what it's called, David. I call it *garbage*.'

David flinched. It was so sad; they didn't understand. He held up his fork, holding a mound of sliced franks and beans. 'Hey, you know, this is pretty good, Dad.'

'Don't change the subject.'

'Cool off, Dad. I don't want to go to church fellowship, and I don't want to go to any of the other things either, because I have to finish my program, *okay?*'

'Cripes, you know, I think that you like that computer of yours better than you like girls. And your mother was worried about the women in your life. There's nothing to worry about. You haven't *got* any.'

David shrugged and swigged some milk. 'Dad, just leave me alone, huh? Get off my case.'

'Just what is it that's so fascinating about computers, David? Just what is the magic of those machines that you can spend hours, *days*, up there, glued to that keyboard and TV set, pumping in numbers and orders, or destroying Space Invaders or whatever it is you do?'

David got up, collected his stuff, and tucked it under his arm.

'Because it's *fun*, Dad.'

'You didn't eat all your dinner, David.'

'Give it to Ralph. He's outside, I think, checking the garbage can.'

With a helpless laugh Harold Lightman looked upward as though toward heaven. 'You know, in the good old days, fathers used to be able to punish their sons by grounding them in their rooms. Doing that to you would be like throwing Brer Rabbit in the briar patch.'

'Yeah, Dad. See ya later.'

In his room, David quickly slid the floppy disk back in the drive, revved up his machines, and got down to serious business. It took him only an hour to figure out the exactly correct sounds and program them into the game. He then saved the subroutine on the master game disk, and made a backup disk, just in case something went kafluey.

Then he played Planet Wreckers.

As the colors flashed, and the spaceships exploded, David Lightman's mind wandered vaguely away from the game. The old man just didn't understand – didn't really *try* to understand. Nobody really cared . . . They were too busy, too wrapped up in their own frozen attitudes, their own games that just kept looping like a faulty program . . .

He finished off the last Earth cruiser with a strong volley of shots. The graphics representing the planet Earth hove into view, lined up in David Lightman's sights.

'You're all *I* need,' he said to his computer system.

He pressed the red button by the joystick. Energy bolts slammed into Earth. Nuclear missiles trailing fire hissed their way toward their targets.

David turned up the volume.

This time, the world ended not only with a bang but with screams and whistles and throbbing explosions and, finally, a mock funeral dirge.

A pounding came on the door. 'David! What the heck was *that*? Are you okay?'

David Lightman turned off his computer and smiled.

Chapter Two

When the wake-up call came, Patricia Healy saw that John McKittrick was already up and dressed. He stood by the hotel room window, gazing out at the Rocky Mountains, smoking a cigarette.

'I've already ordered room service,' he said as Pat put the phone down and struggled to wake up. Not much sleep last night. 'Continental all right for you?'

'Uhmmmmm,' she said, groping for her robe on a nearby chair. 'That's fine, John.' She went to the bathroom. When she came out, John McKittrick was working on a fresh cigarette. She kissed him.

'Thanks,' he said, relaxing a bit in her embrace. 'I needed that.'

'You needed the whole evening,' she said. 'That's why we're in the Colorado Springs Sheraton. Loosen up, you're making me feel like a poor assistant.'

'I'm sorry,' he said, turning and nuzzling her neck, his mustache tickling her. 'I do need you. I do feel better. Dammit, Pat, I'm afraid I'm even in love with you.'

'Yes, well, whatever you are, you're as wired as a piano.' She pulled away to go looking for her clothes. 'It's not as though you haven't made this move before, John. The President knows exactly where you stand.'

'I think there's a chance now,' McKittrick said, stubbing his cigarette out emphatically in an ashtray. 'More than a chance. It's inevitable. Just like I told Falken ... our work would come to this one day!'

'And what did you tell your wife your marriage would come to?'

'Elinor?' McKittrick shook his head sadly. 'She thinks I'm working late down in the Crystal Palace, then bunking there, like dozens of times before.'

'Only you spent the night in the arms of your mistress ... the only woman who understands what's going on in that brilliant, scheming mind of yours.'

'You don't understand either, do you?' McKittrick said.

'I know computers, John,' she said, finding a stocking. 'I know NORAD, I know the defense system. I know my duty and I follow orders as best I can. But it's a job, John. It's not an obsession.'

McKittrick shook his head. 'You didn't know Falken. You're not really appreciative of what he started and what I've improved on ... and could well finish. And it's the *best* sytem, that's just it. Darling, we're still in the 1950s as far as our defense system goes. Don't you see, that's part of the *danger*. Look, I didn't create war and I didn't create nuclear warheads and ICBM missiles or nuclear subs ... and I didn't make Russia or China communist. All Falken and I saw was a terminal situation ... and we acted – or rather *I* acted – to make the North American defense capability the finest possible. And the final stage of our work is within grasp ... today!'

The room service breakfast arrived. Pat Healy sipped coffee and munched on her blueberry Danish, watching as McKittrick tipped the boy.

'You know I'm aware of all that, John,' she said. 'And while I didn't know Falken, I know his work and your work and I believe in it as well. All I'm saying, dear, is that this type-A behaviour is going to give you a heart attack, and I don't want to lose you.'

McKittrick laughed. He sat down beside her on the bed and grabbed a Danish for himself. He was a fortyish man, dark and good-looking and a good boss. Pat had seduced him on a trip to Washington, D.C., almost a year ago, when they'd been there for a round of conferences with Defense Department folk. The first time had been out of curiosity and lust. Now, alas, she was in love with the maniac. Oh, the hazards of the working life . . .

Patricia Healy had received her doctorate in computer science from the University of Maryland after what seemed ages of schooling and student assistantships. When she graduated, it was almost as though the Defense Department had been waiting on her doorstep. Her principal areas of study matched perfectly the specifications of the sort of person they needed. How would you like to work for your country? She wasn't sure about that, but she did like the salary they offered, and the possibility of travel – especially after a failed marriage to an impossible Georgetown law student, and years of being mired in electronic academia. She'd worked in the Pentagon a couple of years, where her work had come to the attention of Dr John McKittrick, distinguished advisor of the Defense Department.

Another job with a larger salary was offered. A move to

Colorado Springs – the location of Cheyenne Mountain sub-terranean headquarters for the North American Air Defense Command – was made, and so here she was, protecting the continent and fooling around with her boss on the side.

'Look, John, you're a marvelous persuader,' she said. 'You know you'll do *fine*. So for heaven's sake, stop worrying. You're going to have those carefully tailored top-echelon Washington bureaucrats in your pocket.'

'You know, you're a truly beautiful woman.'

'And do you love me more than your computers, John?' she asked playfully.

He smiled and messed up her hair. 'Sorry.' He took out another cigarette. 'Make yourself up nice, okay? You're the one who's going to meet Cabot and Watson. I want you to soften them up with your feminine wiles.'

'I thought you said that the forcefulness of your argument would be sufficient.'

'My dear, I need my full complement of armament today . . . and you just happen to be my favorite deadly weapon.'

'Yes, sir,' she said with a mock salute.

Dr John McKittrick, senior advisor to the U.S. Department of Defense, head of NORAD's computer facility, sat alone in a conference room below a hollowed-out mountain, notes and documents spread out before him, waiting impatiently for the arrival of the men from Washington.

Today could be the day he'd waited years for.

Nervously, he checked to make sure he had the video tape of the interview with Captain Hallorhan, the man who'd just failed to carry out the fake command in his North Dakota Minuteman capsule. Statistics were, after all, just statistics.

31

Having a tape of the guy would bring home forcefully to these men the danger of the situation – at which point helpful John A. McKittrick would trot out his simple, elegant solution.

McKittrick went to a window and looked out over the myriad computer consoles and electronic maps of NORAD's combat operations center. The Crystal Palace, they called it, and with good reason. Lights and silicon, silicon and shiny metal, shiny metal and electricity. This was the nerve center for the North American defense system. The one central point that controlled the whole shooting match: submarines and computers, computers and ICBMs, ICBMs and jet bombers ... all carrying their deadly nuclear warheads – capable of destroying the world several times over.

The NORAD command post had once been in a topside building in nearby Colorado Springs – highly vulnerable to enemy attack. In the early 1960s, Cheyenne Mountain was selected as the new base. Tunneling began. Soon there was room for a complex of fifteen steel buildings. This complex soon teemed with computers, communications gear, aerospace technicians and display screens keeping track of all air and space vehicles with sky-sweeping sensors and information from other bases, mobile and static, around the world.

The complex also now housed NORAD's Missile Warning and Space Operations Center, a U.S. office of the Civil Defense National Warning Center, and NORAD's weather support unit. Some seventeen hundred members of the U.S. Navy, Air Force, and Army, along with civilian technicians and Canadian forces, kept the complex functioning on a twenty-four-hour-a-day basis.

For McKittrick, it was home.

He'd helped to design a lot of the computers. They were his children. His and Falken's.

Falken. McKittrick thought about Falken and he smiled to himself. *I'll show you, you stuck-up troublemaker*, he said to the memory. *You just watch.*

Even now those men from Washington in their shiny black Lincoln were probably turning off Colorado Highway 115, making the three-and-a-half-mile, thousand-foot climb to NORAD's entrance, seven thousand feet above sea level.

Pat Healy would meet them at the security gate, distribute red ID tags to clip to their jackets. Then they would travel a third of a mile down a rock-walled tunnel into the man-made grottoes, then through two huge blast doors to the five-acre grid of the complex, each building sitting clear of the rock walls on massive hydraulic shock absorbers. The blast doors were over three feet thick, weighed twenty-five tons each, and were encased in concrete collars. Nonetheless, they could be opened or closed in thirty seconds. The first door was flush against the rock wall so that the heat and blast from a nuclear warhead detonated outside would sweep past, down the tunnel, to exit on the south side of the mountain. There was enough stored food, water, power, and air in the command post to last thirty days if they had to seal it off.

McKittrick had a curiously ambiguous feeling of both safety and anxiety inside this monstrous monument to war. But still it seemed like home.

He was readying the tape player when Pat Healy arrived with their guests. Her lithe brunette charm seemed to have escaped them – they seemed terribly preoccupied, and John McKittrick could not blame them.

McKittrick was familiar with them both, having had correspondence with them and their subordinates. But due to their high ranking, he had never had direct contact. Certainly not a meeting like this one, with so much at stake.

Arthur Cabot's handshake was brisk and brief, as his eyes flicked across the consoles and the gigantic maps in the war room below them. 'Good to finally meet you, McKittrick. Sorry this has to have such a formal setting.'

He was a wrinkled fellow with a crew cut and a double chin. *Leathery* was the word that McKittrick would use to describe him. Tough and leathery ... looking more like a grizzled tank commander than a bureaucrat. His assistant, Lyle Watson, shook hands smoothly, coolly, professionally. Thin and elegant, much younger than Cabot, the man was clearly more suited to playing the diplomat than his boss.

'Gentlemen, please sit down,' said Pat Healy.

'Yes. General Berringer should be here at any moment,' said McKittrick. 'Pat, could you operate the VCR? I've already set it up.'

'Ah! You have the tape we requested,' Cabot said, settling down at the conference table and pouring himself a glass of ice water.

'Shipped here via courier,' McKittrick said. 'A good sample of our problem, I think. Ah – here comes the general.'

General Jack Berringer and his aide Dougherty made a brusque, unhappy entrance. A beefy man, Berringer grumped a reluctant greeting to McKittrick, then made a more formal greeting and introduction with their guests.

That clown knows exactly what I'm up to, McKittrick thought. But there was nothing he could do now to stop him.

'Dr McKittrick,' said Pat Healy. 'I'm ready to roll.'

'Gentlemen,' said McKittrick, sitting at the head of the

table. 'I think we all know why we're here today, so we'll dispense with the briefing. Let it suffice to say that a couple of weeks ago, a routine test of one of our missile commanders, one Captain Jerry Hallorhan of our North Dakota Minuteman silo complex, resulted in Captain Hallorhan's failure to turn his launch key. The captain naturally has been suspended of that duty ... and this tape was made of an interview with him by a trained Air Force psychiatrist.' McKittrick nodded to his assistant. 'Pat – if you would.'

A television monitor was turned on, revealing Captain Hallorhan, a man in his late thirties, muscular, seated in a chair against a blue background. The psychiatrist's voice came from offscreen.

'Have you ever knowingly caused the death of a human being?'

Hallorhan licked his lips. 'I was in Vietnam, sir. I participated in air strikes.'

'But you were younger then ... much younger,' said the psychiatrist.

Hallorhan looked down at his shoes. 'Why is this necessary? I know as an Air Force officer I am pledged by oath to accept without question whatever assignment I'm given. Up to this point, as my records show, I've always performed my duties without question.'

'Then what do you think happened? You had absolutely no idea it was a test?'

'No sir,' Hallorhan replied. 'I thought it was a real strike. I just couldn't make myself turn that key.'

The psychiatrist said, 'Maybe this time you considered the personal moral consequences ... a sense of responsibility ... guilt?'

35

'Maybe so,' Hallorhan said. 'Maybe so.'

Pat Healy rose and turned the sound down on the monitor.

'The interview goes on for another half hour. Apparently this was a case of a man who had last-minute ethical problems. He's not alone. There have been others who simply cannot turn the key ... and they have no explanation why. It's as though they freeze up.'

General Berringer was puffing nervously on a cigar. Its plumes rose up, slowly spreading a bluish pall over the room. 'This man is typical,' he said in a curt professional voice. 'They all have excellent previous records. We just don't pick them at random. It's an *honor* to be a missile commander.'

Cabot sat stiffly. His voice met General Berringer's bluff attitude head on. 'General, over twenty per cent of your missilemen failed or, worse yet, *refused* to launch during the test, like this fellow here. I'd say that so-called honor has very little meaning.'

Watson leaned back in the chair.

'Failure to perform duties is a widespread malaise throughout the armed forces,' he spoke softly to McKittrick. 'But the President is especially concerned about our I CBM capability.'

McKittrick nodded. *Yes, yes, and I'm the man to help you out, folks*, he thought.

Cabot said, 'And we are here because the President wants a solution ... an immediate solution. As you know, the President is not exactly a wimp on the subject of the imperatives of our nation's defense.'

'You can tell the President,' said General Berringer, 'that I have ordered a *complete* review of screening procedures.' He shifted uncomfortably in his seat and put his cigar down in

an ashtray. 'We've called in some big men from the Men-
ninger Clinic.'

McKittrick thought, *Here we go.* 'Excuse me, General,' he
said, 'but I think *that's* a total waste of time. You've picked
good men. The problem is what we're asking them to do.'

Cabot glanced at his watch. 'Look,' he said wearily. 'We've
got to be on a plane in less than an hour. I'm the one who
has to explain to the President why twenty-two per cent of
his missile commanders failed to launch their missiles. What
the hell am I gonna tell him – that twenty-two per cent ain't
so bad? He'll eat me up like a handful of jelly beans!'

Berringer was flustered. 'I'm sure that with the improved
screening procedure –'

'General,' said McKittrick, grabbing for his chance again.
'I don't think we can ask these men to go back to Washington
with a bunch of headshrinking nonsense.' He turned to them
all, pausing dramatically. 'The problem is, you *can't* screen
out human responses. Those men down there know what
turning that key means. What we've got to do, gentlemen,
is to get those men out of the loop.'

Berringer was furious. 'You're out of *line*, McKittrick!'

But Cabot was suddenly perking up. He was clearly intrigued. *You've got him hooked*, thought McKittrick. 'You
mean, take the men out of the launch capsules?'

McKittrick said, 'Why not?'

Berringer stood up, so upset he forgot his cigar. He wagged
his finger at McKittrick. 'We've had men in those silos protecting our country since before any of you were watching
Howdy Doody. I sleep *well* at night knowing those boys are
down there.'

What a turkey, McKittrick thought. 'General,' he countered, calmly and quietly, 'they're fine men, I agree with you there ... but isn't it just a big charade? I mean, all they're supposed to do is turn those keys when the computer tells them to turn the keys.'

'You mean when the President orders them to,' Watson corrected.

'Well, yes,' McKittrick continued. 'But in the event of a nuclear strike, the President would order us to follow the war plan generated by the computer.'

Watson attempted sarcasm, 'I imagine the Joint Chiefs would have some input.'

Berringer grabbed onto that. 'You're damned right they would.'

Cabot shook his head. 'Not a lot, I'm afraid, in this age. If the Soviets launch a surprise attack, we don't have much time.'

Pat Healy looked up. 'Twenty-three minutes from warning till impact. Ten to fifteen minutes if they're sub-launched.'

Good ole Pat, thought McKittrick. *No wonder I love her.* 'Six minutes,' McKittrick said. 'Just enough time for the President to make his decision ... and then it's *all* up to the computers.' He gave them his best sincere look. 'Gentlemen, can you spare five minutes? Let me show you just how it would work.'

Dr John McKittrick walked among his machines like a proud father among children. *Everyone else can hold a Rembrandt painting, or a Flaubert novel, or a Beethoven symphony as pieces of art*, he thought, *but one of these babies will do me just fine.* A field of microchips and relays intricately patterned, meshed into intertwining mechanisms – monuments to genius that didn't just sit there and be beautiful but *worked.*

As they strode along a catwalk, Pat Healy obliged the guests with a tour-guide history of the facility. However, clearly their minds were not on history but rather on the huge banks of computers with their multicolored screens, their blinking lights, the miles and miles of circuitry. The odd technician scurried about like a worker ant in a gigantic hive, while computer men and scientists flipped switches or drank coffee or spoke into their wire headsets below gigantic Mercator maps of North America, of Russia, of China, of the world that glowed in this subterranean dimness, like neon signs in the Times Square night.

'This way, please, gentlemen,' John McKittrick said, guiding his party toward a glass-walled anteroom. Yes, if they accepted his suggestions, finally there would be some true efficiency in the department. And finally he would prove to all these bullheaded military folk what his machines could do. 'If you will just come with me up these steps. Ah, good. Richter is here. Gentlemen, Paul Richter is another of my assistants. Usually you don't work this time, do you, Paul? But I thought it would be wise to have him here to help explain.'

Paul Richter was a sweatered, bespectacled man who looked like the archetypal Freudian psychiatrist, with his goatee and paunch. Nervously, he nodded to the important guests, then leaned against a large gray machine, the size of a VW bug, that flanked a whole lineup of computers.

'Quite a bit of apparatus, Dr McKittrick,' said Cabot, assaying the equipment.

'Mr Cabot, Mr Watson, I presume you know how the information that we act on is obtained,' said McKittrick.

Cabot chuckled, loosening up a bit. 'I believe that's in our job description, isn't it, Watson? Intelligence satellites, re-connaissance planes, reports for agents and stations . . .'

'Quite an intricate network,' Watson put in.

'Yes, and it all funnels in here, to this command post. It goes up on the maps . . .' He paused, then gestured to the banks of blinking lights and tapes that made up the bulk of the room. 'These computers give us instant access to the state of the world. Troop movements . . . Soviet missile tests . . . shifting weather patterns – it all flows into this room' – he walked up to the gray machine where Richter stood fiddling with his black skinny tie – 'and into this . . . the WOPR computer.'

'WOPR?' asked Watson.

'That's War Operation Plan Response.' He turned to his assistant. 'Mr Richter, would you please tell them how it works.'

A ghost of a smile crept to Richter's lips, then vanished. 'Well.' He cleared his voice, obviously more used to com-muning with computers than communicating with humans. 'The WOPR spends its time thinking about World War III twenty-four hours a day, three hundred and sixty-five days a year. It plays an endless series of war games, using all available information on the state of the world.'

McKittrick continued. 'The WOPR has already fought World War III as a *game* any number of times, estimating Soviet responses and so on. Then it looks for ways to improve its score in a real war. The point is, the key decisions about every conceivable option in a nuclear crisis have already been made by the WOPR. If the day ever comes when the President orders us to follow the plans, I want to make damn sure they're carried out. The point is, this little baby is the best general we've got, the best wager of war. Should the awful event of a nuclear war be necessary, this fellow will be able to fight it with a great margin of hope for *victory*.'

Cabot nodded, clearly sympathetic. 'What you're saying is that our system right now – all this trillion-dollar hardware that we need so desperately – is at the mercy of those men with the little brass keys with an incredible rate of failure.'

'The only problem, sir, is that they're *human*. And sir, with all due respect, are any of us sure that if we had their jobs, we'd be able to twist those keys and snuff out millions of lives?' He looked around. Watson coughed, McKittrick stared straight at Cabot. This was the punch line. 'You give me four to six weeks max and we can replace those men – mere fallible human mechanisms anyway – with highly dependable electronic relays. We can get the humans out of the loop!'

Berringer interrupted with his usual lack of grace: 'I've told you, John, I don't trust this overgrown pile of microchips any farther than I can throw it. You're talking about eliminating human control. I grant you, nobody in our military can match it for nuclear war experience. But we look to it only as an advisor.'

McKittrick countered, 'But once that advice is given, and if, God forbid, the President must act on it, there is just no time for any fumbles between him and our defense forces for the war to be fought properly. We'll keep the human control ... but where it belongs ... at the top.'

Cabot pondered for a moment, then said, 'Dr McKittrick, this is all so technical ... I think it might be best if you personally briefed the President on your views.'

'Certainly,' said McKittrick. 'I'd be happy to.'

He smiled over at General Berringer, who grimaced.

Cabot said, 'Yes. Well, other than the jerking of a few liberal knees, I don't see any problem in actually implementing your suggestion.' He stepped forward and halted, his hand just above the machine. 'May I touch it?'

'Sure,' McKittrick said. 'Go ahead.'

Well, Falken, he thought. *I told you that one of these days I'd get my way. All this will truly be mine now. I'll get the recognition I deserve. So bug off, you has-been genius. Just bug off.*

Cabot seemed fascinated with the machine. 'So, this is where Armageddon is played,' he said, putting his ear to the machine. 'I think I hear the bombs bursting.'

Chapter Three

David Lightman hovered over the controls of the Atari Missile Command tucked neatly between the Frogger machine and the Zaxxon game. Tony was pounding dough by the ovens, listening to Pat Benatar shriek about false loves through a beat-up radio. The smell of a fresh pie drifted warmly through Marino's Pizza Shop, so thick you could almost taste the cheese. David Lightman, carelessly dressed in the torn T-shirt and faded jeans he'd tossed on this morning, was oblivious to it all, however, aware only of the booms and rattles and whistles, the flashing colored lights of the game.

Darned Smart Bombs! he thought as a white buzzing blip snuck through his latest volley of shots and headed for one of his six cities at the bottom of the screen. He spun the control ball, stitched a neat three-*X* line just below the descending bomb with the cursor, and watched with immense satisfaction as his missiles streaked white lines to their targets, blowing the bomb right out of the phosphor-dot sky.

As the machine added up his points and the color of the screen changed, he noted with satisfaction that he still had six bonus cities as backup, should one of the enemy bombs make it all the way down this time. And he had racked up over two hundred thousand points! All the initials of the top ten for this machine were going to be DAL real soon now!

A troublesome thought occurred to him. He checked the time on his Bulova digital watch. Yikes – 1:06 P.M.! Lunch hour was kaput, and he was late for his fourth-period class!

He turned around to see if that kid he'd noticed peripherally watching him was still hanging around. Yep, there he was, eyes round in a freckled face. 'Geez, man, you're *great*,' the kid said. Tomato sauce had given him a red mustache.

'You wanna finish for me?'

'You bet!'

'Go ahead.'

Grabbing up his books, David Lightman rushed out of the snack bar and hustled toward Hubert Humphrey High. The sky above Seattle looked like it was about ready to cut loose with some serious wet. Of course, that was typical for Seattle.

He raced past the duplexes and the town houses and cut across a well-manicured lawn, much like every well-manicured lawn of any American suburb. Sometimes he wondered what it would be like to live in California or Florida or Kansas or anyplace else in the United States, but in the end he realized that they were all pretty much the same, and since he'd lived in Washington all his life, his father ensconced in a mildly profitable certified public accountant job, his mother discovering the joys of real estate, Seattle would have to do for a while longer.

Humphrey High was a series of gray boxes strewn geometrically at a busy crossroads, surrounded by a useless mesh fence. David slipped under the much-used 'secret en-

44

trance' – a section where the mesh had been clipped – and shot through the side entrance. Recklessly ignoring any hall monitors, he ran downstairs to where the homerooms and the chemistry and biology labs were located, found Room Fourteen, and then slowed to a casual saunter for his entrance.

The place reeked of formaldehyde, animals, and fertilizer. Aquariums bubbled. A hamster wheel squeaked. The teacher, one Amos Ligget, stood by the blackboard, a piece of chalk gripped in a chubby hand.

'Ah!' he said, noting the new arrival. 'So glad you could join us, David.' He wiped back a clump of limp hair from his eyes and waddled to the black-countered lab table that walled him from his students. 'Little present for you here!'

David had already started for the back. Whenever possible he sat in the back of the class, keeping a low profile, yearning for obscurity. He halted, turned around, and went back to Ligget, who stood holding a blue test book displayed so that all the class could see it. That jerk! One of the key weapons of sadistic teachers was public humiliation, and Ligget wielded it like Conan the Barbarian wielded his broadsword – and about as subtly. Scrawled on the cover of the book, vivid as Hawthorne's Scarlet Letter they were reading about now in American lit, was a red-inked *F*.

Ligget was smiling, showing faintly yellow teeth. A scattering of dandruff lay on his black polyester coat. The students called Ligget 'Atom Bomb' sometimes because he had so much fallout.

David took the book, his whole manner an eloquent shrug.

He made his way to a desk and noted with some astonishment that the one by Jennifer Mack was empty. He sat, a little

45

excited. He made a point of not staring at her, stiffly directing his attention back to Ligget, who now displayed another crimson *F* on a blue book.

Oh yeah, old Ligget is feeling his oats today, David thought as the bulky man wandered before the class, waxing lyrical. 'Question four! In the history of science, novel and innovative concepts occasionally come from sudden left-field inspiration.' He leaned against the table, his soft belly spilling onto the Formica. 'Jennifer? Ah! There you are! Jennifer Mack, in answering question number twenty-four, "Why do nitrogen nodules cling to the roots of plants? . . ."'

David turned to his classmate. Her hazel eyes were turned down in embarrassment, letting a sweep of brunette hair touch the desk top. Nice hair, soft and glistening. Absently, David wondered what hair like that felt like to the touch.

Ligget continued, unmercifully, '. . . You have written the word *Love*.'

The class turned around and looked at her, tittering. A wave of sympathy shot through David.

'Love indeed, Miss Mack,' the jerk was grinning, enjoying himself. 'Miss Mack, is there perhaps something you know about nitrogen nodules that we don't? Some bit of salacious info to which you alone are privy?'

Jennifer looked up and met his glance, almost defiantly. 'No,' she said. David had never seen her look prettier.

'I see.' Ligget turned away from her direct gaze. 'You didn't know the correct answer – symbiosis – because you don't pay attention in class.' Ligget made sure everyone saw Jennifer's grade, then tossed it contemptuously to a student in the first row. 'Would you please pass this to Miss Mack.'

Jennifer sighed. She noticed that David was looking at her,

remembered that he had not laughed. She smiled at him. He sensed a warmth and vulnerability in her that coaxed a response in him. 'Don't worry. *F* could mean "fantastic".'

'Uh uh,' she whispered. '*F* stands for the fanny my dad's going to paddle when he gets a load of my grades.'

Ligget sallied onward, discussing more of the dreadful exam. 'Now, on the questions that concerned the definition of cloning, there seemed to be some confusion.' He looked entreatingly at the class. 'Can somebody tell me who first suggested the idea of an advance organism reproducing asexually?'

He turned to the blackboard and began chalking up some words. David turned away from Jennifer, relieved that he didn't have to continue the conversation. He had problems with girls. Not that he didn't like them. They were just such unknown factors. Variables, computer language might call them, although girls didn't follow any kind of logical behavior. Knuckling under to peer pressure, he'd taken a few out to movies, but he shunned the dances and the mixers. He felt clumsy and awkward at the best of times, but those affairs were worse than the Spanish Inquisition. The thing was, he felt like he had no control of the situation with girls ... not like his computer. He didn't understand the way he felt when they were around, smiling at him. He almost felt *embarrassed* at how he wanted to touch them.

God, if only he knew how to talk to someone like Jennifer Mack. She smiled at him a lot, especially since that day old Ligget had brought in the boa.

They'd been discussing reptiles, and the next thing David knew, a tank had found its way onto Ligget's gigantic lab table. It was a glass tank, containing a six-foot-long boa

47

constrictor, as thick around in the middle as the right bicep on Hank Jodrey, the star wrestler. A truly evil-looking thing, it had slithered around, glaring at them, flicking its tongue as though it were hungrily licking its chops. Most of the girls sat in the rear of the class that week.

One day, though, old Ligget topped himself. He hauled fat Herman, the class hamster, out of his cage, unclamped the wire top of the snake tank, and popped the rodent in with the boa. 'I have to run an errand, class. I want a full report on what happens here.'

As he left, the whole class grimaced in horror. The snake had been wound up in a pile in the corner, asleep, but when that little golden fellow started scampering around on the newspaper, Mr B. C. took distinct notice.

Most of the guys got fascinated smirks on their faces, watching what was going to happen. David, however, was disgusted. Without a word he raced up to the teaching dais, lifted the top of the snake tank, reached in, and yanked Herman out. The girls had applauded.

'Hey, Lightman. You're gonna get in trouble!' a creep named Crosby said.

'You tell, John,' his girl friend said, 'and you can forget Friday night!'

'What are we gonna tell Atom Bomb?' someone wanted to know.

'Tell him that the snake ate Herman,' suggested somebody.

'But there won't be any bulge.'

'The turkey forgot his glasses today.'

Jennifer smiled at him that day for the first time, and Herman was in the corner of his room now, safe from boa constrictors.

48

ASEXUAL REPRODUCTION = WITHOUT SEX, read the scrawl on the blackboard.

A few chuckles spread through the class, though nothing like the roar Peter Hawkins had gotten when he'd accidentally pronounced *organism* as *orgasm* last week.

'I fail to see the humor in this,' Ligget said. 'Mr Rudway, would *you* please tell me who first suggested the idea of an advanced organism reproducing asexually.'

Rudway moved uncomfortably in his seat. 'Mendel?'

'A bit early.'

David grinned, his eyes lighting up. He leaned over toward Jennifer and whispered two words to her.

Jennifer snorted. She tried to keep it in, but even her hand over her mouth couldn't contain her loud chortles.

Annoyed, Ligget said, 'Miss Mack, are you having an epileptic fit? Just what is so funny?'

Jennifer kept her head down, seeming to gain control of herself. But then she looked over at David and cracked up again.

Ligget was incensed, and just like a shark, he wouldn't let go. 'All right Lightman. Maybe *you* can tell us who first suggested reproduction without sex,' he demanded, his face mottled red.

David straightened, glanced at Jennifer, lifting an eyebrow John Belushi style, then turned and smiled at old Atom Bomb.

'Your wife?' he said.

'Mr Ligget wants me to discuss an attitude problem with Mr Kessler,' David Lightman said in his best Hi-here-I-am-again-in-the-vice-principal's-office voice.

Mrs Mitchell, a young woman, looked skeptically up at him from above her half frames. 'I do believe I've seen you here before.'

She buzzed him through, and turned back to her typewriter, wielding a Liquid Paper brush like Picasso.

David Lightman dragged on through the door into a short corridor. He plopped down on the hard wooden bench and stared intently at his scruffy Adidas.

Hey, he thought. *You know, as long as I'm here . . .*

He smiled to himself and checked on Mrs Mitchell. Out of view. Good. He peered down the hallway. To the immediate right, of course, was the 'Kaiser's' office, Discipline Center of Humphrey High. A stern voice barked behind a closed door.

At the far end of the room were the school's two computer rooms. David could see that in one a middle-aged woman bent over a terminal. But the other room, door wide open, was empty.

Hot *dog*! Just as he'd hoped. Jennifer was a good foil. He just prayed that the user password was displayed.

Keeping a wary eye on the woman in the other room, David darted toward the deserted computer room. This stunt sure could play hell with his relationships with the high mucky-mucks at Hubert Humphrey High, but it was worth the strain.

It was but the work of a second.

Taped to the monitor housing was a long list of six-letter words, all crossed out but the last: *pencil*.

Far out!

David dashed back to the bench, sitting just as the VP's door opened, discharging a cowed-looking student who scampered off like a guilty dog.

'Kaiser' Kessler motioned David in. 'Well, Lightman. What a surprise.'

David moped in, proffering the note from Ligget.

Kessler accepted the note, scanned it, then leaned back in his chair, pursing his thick lips as he surveyed David Lightman thoughtfully.

'You know, Lightman, I can't figure you,' he said. 'Go on, sit down. I want to talk. No essays this time, no note to your parents, no call to your pop.'

Suspicious, David Lightman sat down.

'You have excellent SATs ... particularly in math ... yes, I checked with your counselor.' Kessler wore his hair in a crew cut. In his late thirties, he looked like a German drill instructor, which was why the students called him 'Kaiser'. His fame as a disciplinarian was known throughout the school system, not necessarily for its effectiveness but for the real glee that Kessler seemed to take in his job. David suspected that the man actually regretted living in the 1980s and wished he ruled his roost in the era of paddles and canes. He'd make a great Dickens character.

'So?'

'You are a prime candidate for becoming a sterling student, and yet I see you in here time and time again.'

'Gee, Mr Kessler, I don't beat up on kids and I don't drink or smoke or do drugs ...'

'You're just a smart aleck ... you just annoy the hell out of your teachers ...' Kessler chuckled and put his hands behind his head. 'Now what kind of school would we have if everyone was a smart aleck, Lightman?'

'A school of bright bums?'

Kessler laughed. 'You know, if you were my boy, Lightman, I'd take you over my knee and brighten *your* bum. But then, I suspect it's too late. It's not an easy job these days to be a teacher, Lightman. Class disrupters make it all the more difficult for teachers.'

'Yes, sir.'

'You're a know-it-all, aren't you, Lightman? You think you can have it your way at all times. You like to throw sticks in the wheels just to see a cog or two break. Oh, you're not a bad kid. I know bad kids, believe me. Still and all, you're a little perverse, aren't you?' Kessler smiled as he took a toothpick from its pack and began cleaning his teeth. 'You know, don't you, Lightman, that I'm in charge of the activities room.'

David blinked.

'Yes, well, it happens I am now and I have a little note here ... my goodness, it's an official request from one David Lightman requesting video games for the room. Well now, Lightman, some of the teachers think that this is a fine idea, but I just read the Surgeon General's report on how very *bad* those things are for people – Pac-Man elbow, strained eyes, tendencies toward violence – and your coming in here like this, a perfect example of what video games do to the adolescent mind, makes me realize that the last thing I want to see in my activities rooms are video games.'

Kessler tore up David's letter and tossed it in the garbage.

'Filed in the round file, Lightman. Now get out of here, and don't let me see you here again.'

Kessler turned his slightly protuberant eyes back to the papers on his desk.

'Yes, sir.'

52

Sieg heil would be a better response for that creep. The other kids could call him 'Kaiser', but from now on in David Lightman's book he was *Führer* all the way.

The thing was, most of the people in charge, in positions of authority, were such complete turkeys, David Lightman thought as he left another scintillating day at Humphrey High behind him, walking home listlessly, a single book – trig – riding in his palm.

It wouldn't be so bad if they *knew* they were turkeys. David knew gobble-speak pretty good, he realized that. No, they all thought they were big deals, were better than he was . . . better than everybody. Thought they were in control of things, thought they knew the score on everything.

That was the nice thing about computers. With computers, you got justice. What you put in, you got out. Instant results. All the rest of this world . . . well, it was as gray as the sky riding above Seattle now.

The sound of a small motor hummed behind him. David Lightman waited for the Doppler effect when the scooter passed him, but instead the sound stayed steady, pacing him. He turned. There on a green moped was Jennifer Mack, riding along beside him.

'Hi!' she said.

'Oh, hi,' returned David.

David turned away; there was nothing much to say. He tried to turn his tongue-tiedness into something he hoped would pass for Clint Eastwood coolness.

Jennifer said, 'I'm sorry I got you in trouble. I just couldn't stop laughing.'

Good grief, she was apologizing for helping him out. He

slowed down and looked at her. 'No. It's okay. You were perfect.'

Jennifer stopped the moped, her face incredulous. 'I was?'

'Uh huh.'

She was a slim, shapely girl, dressed today in jeans, a green surf-shirt, and a black Windbreaker. A breeze tossed a few strands of her long hair around recklessly. The expression on her face now was really cute. David didn't know what to say to her.

Jennifer was the one to break the awkward silence. 'Hey. You want a ride home?' she asked brightly.

'Sure,' David said automatically.

'Hop on, then!' she invited.

'Uh ... right.' David carefully sat down on the back of the moped, one hand hooking on the bottom of Jennifer's seat. 'I'm set.'

'Where do you live?'

'Not far.' He gave her quick instructions.

'Hang on, here we go!'

Jennifer Mack proceeded to mix with the Seattle suburban traffic, mostly to David's chagrin. A Volkswagen beeped at them. David choked on a plume of exhaust. They bounced over a bump, and he felt like he was about to fall off. Cripes, she was going too fast!

As she made an Evel Knievel turn onto Elm, David's feet dragged on the asphalt.

Jennifer turned and shouted over her shoulder, 'Hey! Lift those knees.'

David lifted his knees.

'And for goodness' sake, sit closer! I'm not going to bite!'

David gingerly put his hands on her waist. Her sides were smooth and firm.

'That's no good. I don't want to have to turn around and pick up your pieces,' she said impatiently.

David swallowed. He slipped his arms all the way around Jennifer; the feeling was indescribable. The wind whipped her hair back into his face. It was silkier than he imagined, and it smelled clean and perfumey.

You know, he thought. *Computers can't do* this.

On a free stretch of road without many cars, Jennifer said, 'Hey! You got an F too, huh?'

Geez, she was really *warm*. 'Yup,' he said absently.

'Yeah. I guess we'll both be stuck in summer school.'

David had to smile at that. 'Not me!'

'Why not? Aren't you going to have to make up biology?'

Not if that password was correct, David thought smugly. 'I don't think so.'

Jennifer paused, clearly confused. 'Why *not?*'

'If you'll come into my house, I'll show you!'

'Sure. Why not?'

David pointed up the road, feeling rather sorry now that this ride couldn't be longer. 'It's up there.'

Through the overcast spring day, under green oaks, past hedge-lined residences, the little moped hummed along. David indicated the house, and Jennifer pulled up beside it. David hopped off as Jennifer turned the moped off and supported it on its kickstand.

David turned in time to intercept Ralph, who bounded down the slight slope in front of the house to greet the newcomers.

'Your dog?' Jennifer said.

'Yeah,' said David, giving the setter a quick roughhouse pet. 'Name's Ralph. This is Jennifer, Ralph. She's okay.'

Ralph's ears pricked up. He pranced over to Jennifer and began to sniff her, then he jumped up on her in an overly familiar fashion.

Embarrassed, David yelled, 'Ralph!'

'That's okay,' Jennifer said. 'I have a dog too.' She gently pushed Ralph away, petting him. 'Dogs don't have to take biology.'

'Uh ... yeah,' David said, grabbing Ralph by the chain around his neck. Ralph yelped. 'C'mon, pal. Be good. This is a *guest*, you mutt! Sorry, but you're gonna have to stay outside.'

Jennifer laughed and he led her past the ceramic flamingoes into the two-storey house. Inside it was deserted, the downstairs still smelling from the bacon his father had burned that morning.

Looking around, Jennifer suddenly seemed a bit nervous. She paused, and David turned around.

'Uh ... what I have to show you is in my room. And ...' He was suddenly aware of the situation he'd put them in. 'My ... uh ... room. It's upstairs.'

Jennifer shrugged off her caution and followed him. 'Your parents aren't home?' she asked halfway up the stairs. There was a strange tone in her voice, as though she were a little excited about something.

David's heart started to pitter-pat. 'They both work.' What did she think he was up to? He just wanted to show her the computer.

Jennifer followed him, silently. But she laughed at the sign on his door. '"This is a secure area",' she read aloud.

'"Authorized entry only. No exception". What do I need, David, some kind of pass?'

Taking out a key, David said. 'Naw. I'll turn off the booby traps.' He unlocked the door and motioned her in.

'It's pitch black!' she objected, hesitating.

'Oh. Just a minute.' He leaned through and snapped on the lights. Yikes! The place was a mess. He'd forgotten that.

Jennifer didn't seem to notice, though. She breezed past him, astonished at the array of machinery David had set up in his room.

Still embarrassed, David spotted a pile of dirty underwear and socks. Edging along with Jennifer, he kicked the pile under the unmade bed.

'Wow. You're really into computers, huh?'

'Yeah. That's what I wanted to show you.'

'But what's that got to do with my biology grade, for goodness' sake?' Jennifer asked, eyes still drifting over the bewildering array of wires and gadgets, as though she were in a flying saucer.

'Here. I'll show you right now.'

David slipped past her, settling in the torn swivel chair. He turned on the terminal, then warmed up the TV. *Now, where the heck was that stupid modem? Ah, there.* He reached for the telephone coupler situated by the phone, then stuck the receiver into its cradle.

He checked a phone book full of scrawls, found the number he was looking for, then punched it out on the push buttons.

'What are you doing?' Jennifer asked softly.

'I'm dialing into the central school district's system, and if we're lucky . . . Yep, it's available.'

On the monitor a flash of words appeared:

THIS IS THE GREATER SEATTLE UNIFIED SCHOOL
DISTRICT DATANET.
PLEASE LOG IN WITH USER PASSWORD AND
ACCOUNT NUMBER.

'You see, Jennifer,' David continued. 'They change the
password every couple of weeks.' He paused for dramatic
effect. 'But *I* know where they write it down!'

David tapped the word *pencil* onto the keyboard.

Immediately the screen wiped and displayed a list of
subsystems to choose from.

'Go ahead, Jennifer, just type out the words *student transcripts.*'

'No. I don't ...'

David smiled. 'Ah c'mon. The computer won't bite.' He
was in his element now, and he felt much more at ease. She
stepped forward, found the right keys, and typed.

STUDENT TRANSCRIPTS appeared on the screen.

'There we go. Now, I'll just key in my student ID number
... and *voilà*,' David proclaimed. 'Behold my dismal grades.'
The screen wiped, and suddenly there, in black and white,
were the records for one LIGHTMAN, DAVID A.

David moved the cursor over to the biology grade, and
changed the *F* to a *C*.

'What are you *doing*?' Jennifer asked, horrified.

'Just changing my grade ... now what's your ID
number?'

Jennifer muttered some letters, and David typed them out.

Immediately the transcripts for MACK, JENNIFER D.
appeared.

David peered at it.

What David was up to finally seemed to register on Jennifer. 'Hey . . . you can't *do* this!'

'Why not? It's easy.'

'This is none of your business. What are you doing now?'

'I'm changing your biology grade.'

'Wait a minute. You're going to get me in trouble,' Jennifer protested.

'Relax. No one will find out. Watch!'

David took the cursor over to the biology grade, where he efficiently transformed an *F* into a *B*.

'You just got a B, Jennifer. Now you don't have to go to summer school.'

'Change it back,' Jennifer demanded.

David was dumbstruck. 'Why? I promise you. They can't possibly trace . . .'

'I said, change it back!' Jennifer was clearly extremely upset.

David said, 'Okay! Okay!'

He punched the *F* key. 'There you go. You now have an F again.'

Jennifer coolly backed away. 'Listen, I guess I better get going.'

'Sure.' David, stood up, confused. 'Thanks again for the ride.'

'Yeah. Okay.' She backed away, then fled. ' 'Bye.'

'Don't you want me to walk you . . . ?' David said, but Jennifer was already gone. David went to the window and watched her run to her moped. She peddled it to a start, then *varoomed* down the street.

'Girls,' David muttered, a sinking feeling in the pit of his stomach. Still, Jennifer was a pretty nice one. David guessed that he hadn't introduced her to the idea of fooling with computers this way slowly enough. She was too locked into social programming that said the authorities made the rules and you can't fool around with them, even if you're cleverer than the numbskulls who told you how you were supposed to be.

The thing was, David didn't really care about his biology grade. It was just a convenience. What he got the most satisfaction out of was playing around behind those dummies' backs, thumbing his nose at them, and *they didn't even know it!*

It gave David Lightman an immense amount of pure, unadulterated delight.

He hopped over to his computer, changed Jennifer's Biology F back to a B, then quickly bailed out of the datanet before anyone caught his greasy hands in the works.

In the den, Cathy Lee Crosby, Fran Tarkenton, and John Davidson crooned 'That's Incredible!' from the TV set, which segued into a C. and P. Telephone Company commercial.

David Lightman slipped a dollop of creamed chipped beef to Ralph, who waited patiently under the dinner table. He wiped his hand on a paper napkin, then returned to the junk mail scattered to his right.

Ralph, sensing that no more snacks would be coming from David, wagged his way over to Mr Lightman, who sat meticulously buttering a piece of corn, using a slice of bread to distribute the butter evenly.

A full plate of food lay cooling before another chair. Mrs Lightman had gotten a real estate call early in the meal.

'But you've got to see the place,' she was chattering over

the phone in the kitchen. 'It's the pride and joy of all my listings. Yes, two bedrooms, a bath and a half, and a huge bonus room.'

'Ralph!' said Mr Lightman as Ralph began to drip saliva on his pants leg. 'You already ate! Now stay.'

David sifted through the mail absently. Only real thing of interest here was his new *Cool Computer* magazine.

'David, did you put out the trash?' his father asked.

'Yeah, yeah,' David said wearily. His father had asked him that twice so far this evening.

His mother cupped her hand over the phone's mouthpiece, and cried out, 'Now honey, put the lid on real tight so Ralph won't turn it over again.' The she turned back to her wheeling and dealing.

'I know, Mom.' Sheesh. If they weren't ignoring him, they were nagging him. He flipped through *Cool Computer* casually. As he turned the middlemost pages, an insert fell into his lap.

Whoa ho! What was this!

In vivid blues and reds crisscrossed with futuristic-style lettering, the flyer proclaimed: QUANTUM LEAP IN COMPUTER GAMES FROM PROTOVISION THIS SUMMER

David quickly finished his dinner, washed it down with some milk, and then excused himself.

Protovision was in California. It was worth a try.

He hopped toward his room, past his mother.

'One of these days,' she said, noting the magazine in his hand, 'you're going to electrocute us all!'

'Yeah,' David said into his phone. 'Sunnyvale, California. Protovision. Thanks.' A thought crossed his mind. 'Oh, and could you tell me what other prefixes cover that area?'

He jotted the numbers down on a pad.

'Thank you!'

Hauling out a small plastic file-box, David Lightman flipped through a number of black, sleeved disks the size of 45 rpm records. These were his floppies – floppy disks, magnetic storage units for programs. And to think that years ago, when he first started, he was using a cassette deck and tape. These things were faster to boot up, easier to save programs on, easier to load. This particular box was filled with programs of his own devising. Another box on the other side of the room held 'backups' – exact copies. The only problem with floppies was that sometimes, if the computer crashed, or there was a power surge, or you bent the damned thing, you could forget what you had stored on it.

He pulled out one labeled

MODEM TONE SCAN
COPYRIGHT BY DAVID LIGHTMAN
UNAUTHORIZED USE OR DUPLICATION
OF THIS PROGRAM IS STRICTLY
PROHIBITED.

David had gotten his modem almost a year ago. The first month he had used it, he had racked up a truly incredible phone bill. So after that, David Lightman had gotten real interested in the workings of the telephone company. His friend Jim Sting had helped him out on that one. Old Sting hated the phone company too. Sting had a pile of information. In his heyday the computer expert had been a Phone

Phreak – a prankster who used his knowledge of computers to get toll free phone calls.

Yeah, Sting had even helped him on this program.

He'd done this before, finding the telephone number for computers, raiding them. It was fun. All he had to do was to get in contact with the Protovision computer, use his other special software to get past any safeguard, call up these new games, and copy them onto a couple of floppies.

He'd have them before anybody else!

In goes the phone, into the modem . . .

A tap of the keyboard's return key . . .

TO SCAN FOR MODEM TONES, PLEASE LIST DESIRED AREA CODE AND PREFIX.

David typed in: 311-399, 311-437, 311-767, 311-936.

Automatically the computer dialed the first number.

From the receiver David could hear a faint ring. An irate voice answered, 'Hello.'

No go. The computer was searching for the tones used by another modem to answer calls. Immediately the computer disconnected the call.

It rang the next number.

From previous experience David knew that the process could take *hours*. These computer folks weren't dumb. They didn't exactly hand out their special modem numbers on a silver platter. With a nation full of hackers, that would be tantamount to suicide.

The monitor screen began to fill up with numbers. *Good job*, David thought. *Good job.*

After turning down the monitor speaker, he grabbed a new science fiction paperback he'd shoplifted – a novel called *Day of the Dragonstar* – and began to read.

Chapter Four

David Lightman dodged Speedy, faked out Pinky, then rounded the corner and headed straight for the power dot.

Gulp.

The ghosts turned blue. David grinned. He'd maneuvered them perfectly. Zap, zap, zap, zap, he ate them all up with Pac-Man. He took the moment's respite to reach over for his slice.

Jennifer Mack stood by the table, sipping at a Tab. 'Hi.'

'Oh, hi.'

David turned back to the machine, eating more dots. The ghosts were on the move again, and the buggers were fast now.

'You're gonna spoil your dinner,' Jennifer said.

'This is my dinner.'

'Listen, I thought it over last night.'

'What?' Yikes, they were closing in, and only one power dot left on this screen.

'That thing with my grade. Can you still change it?'

David lost his concentration, made the wrong move in this pattern. Clyde eagerly grabbed him. Pac-Man faded away with a despairing whine.

'I can't believe I was so stupid. I should have just let you do it.' She looked at the game. 'Hey, you're really good. I didn't know that Pac-Man went that high. I can't break thirty thousand.'

Pac-Man was on the move again, and David steered him expertly. He gobbled up a fruit and the machine made a silly noise.

'Anyway,' Jennifer continued doggedly. 'I wanted to ask you if you could still do it.'

Cripes, thought David Lightman. Women. His mom was like that sometimes, changing her mind right in the middle of a sentence. David dodged Inky and escaped through one side, re-emerging on the other.

'Uh, I don't know. It might be kinda rough.'

'Why?'

'Uh, I don't know. They might have changed the password.'

Jennifer was sweet but insistent. 'But maybe they didn't. Could we at least try and see?'

He visualized her back in his bedroom, and suddenly Pinky caroomed down a maze corridor and grabbed him.

He looked over at Jennifer, annoyed.

But her eyes were so very pretty when they pleaded.

'Please?' she said.

The guy was kinda weird, but he was kinda cute, too, in a kooky way, and, well, if he really could fix her grade so that she wouldn't have to go to summer school, then that was fine by Jennifer Mack.

His parents were gone again.

'What's your mom do?' she asked, munching on some Juicy Fruit as he let them in.

'Century 21.'

'Huh?'

'Real estate.'

'Oh.' She glanced around at the living room, which was much like her living room and a dozen other living rooms she'd seen. At least it didn't have plastic on the cushions, she thought as she followed David up to the room.

'Hey, I forgot. How's Herman?'

'Fine. I use his wheel now to power my stuff.'

She laughed. 'Your Phase X modified prefontal disco-driver with detachable trash compactor?'

'Yeah. My computer. C'mon. It's been working on something all day.'

He took out his keys and commenced to unlock his bedroom door. Two dozen guys in her school had asked her up to their bedrooms, and she'd turned them down. So here she was trotting up to Dipsy Dave's room for the second time, and after he fixed her grade, they'd probably end up playing Space Invaders.

You know, he really wasn't bad-looking, in a sallow, skinny kinda way. Jennifer wondered what it would be like to neck with him. Fun, maybe.

The room was lit eerily by the TV set. David turned on the lights as Jennifer wandered over and looked at the screen. It looked like the thing was printing out phone numbers.

'What's it doing?' she asked.

'Don't touch the keys,' David said.

She flinched away from the keyboard. 'I won't, but, like, what's it *doing?*'

She stepped aside and let David sit down. He answered her absently, his attention fixed in fascination on his computer system. She was so interested in his answer herself, she didn't even notice the sour male smell of the room this time.

'Dialing numbers,' David was saying. 'This California computer company – Protovision – is coming out with these amazing new games in a couple of months. The programs for them are probably still in their computer, so I told my system to search for computers in Sunnyvale.' He took the phone out of its contraption, and handed it to her. Now *phones* Jennifer Mack understood. She put the earpiece automatically to her ear. 'The computers I get answer with a tone that other computers can recognize.'

Jennifer took the phone from her ear. Just a tone there. The list of phone numbers was piling up. 'You're calling every number in Sunnyvale, California?'

David turned to her with a self-satisfied grin.

'Isn't that expensive?'

'There's ways around that!' David said, true glee in his eye.

This fellow was a real maniac, Jennifer thought. Cute but crazy. 'Like, is this going to take long? I'd really like to get my grade changed.'

'Yeah,' David said, eyes glued to the TV set. 'Well, the thing is, Jennifer. Actually, I, uh ... already changed it.'

'What! I told you not to do that!'

'I was sure you'd change your mind.'

Well, of all the nerve!

'Besides, I didn't want you to flunk.' He was suddenly off the subject of her grade and back into his trance. 'Let's see what we've got so far.'

He tapped one of the keys, and the TV read:

UNION MARINE BANK, SOUTHWEST BRANCH HEADQUARTERS.

LOG IN, PLEASE.

'Got to remember that one,' David said. 'Might come in handy someday.'

Jennifer suddenly became more interested. She moved closer.

David typed in another number and got the Department of Motor Vehicles.

'Got any tickets in Sunnyvale?'

'You mean if I had a speeding ticket, you could fix it?'

David shrugged as he punched up the next number and said, 'Probably.' The screen filled up with cities, dates, flight numbers. It was Pan Am flight listings.

Jennifer said, 'Oh, good. Let's go somewhere.'

This wasn't what David was looking for, but Jennifer looked hooked. 'Where do you want to go?' he said.

'Paris. It's so romantic.'

Two quick keystrokes and David looked up to say, 'Okay, we're booked.' As soon as he hit another key, more numbers spewed. Jennifer watched. Suddenly the numbers were gone and the screen just read:

LOG ON.

David said, 'Geez, that's strange. It doesn't identify itself. Let's try . . . anything.'

He typed in a bunch of zeroes and a one.

The TV responded with:

IDENTIFICATION NOT RECOGNIZED BY SYS-TEM. YOU HAVE BEEN DISCONNECTED.

'That's pretty rude,' Jennifer said, quite involved by now.

'I'll ask it to help me log on,' David said, redialing the number.

'Can you do that?'

'Sure. Some systems will help you out. The more complicated they are, the more they *have* to!'

LOG ON.

HELP LOG ON.

HELP NOT AVAILABLE. LOG ON.

Jennifer was vexed. 'Now what?'

David was clearly excited. 'You know, I think this *might* be Protovision. And if it *is* . . .'

HELP GAMES, David typed.

The monitor replied immediately:

GAMES REFERS TO MODELS, SIMULATIONS, AND GAMES WHICH HAVE TACTICAL AND STRATEGIC APPLICATIONS.

David whooped, 'Yeah! I think we've got 'em. Turn that printer on, would you? Let's get a printout of this.'

Enjoying herself as assistant to the mad scientist, Jennifer went to the IBM I that David indicated and hit the 'on' switch.

LIST GAMES, David requested.

The TV set stayed blank.

'C'mon. C'mon, c'mon!' David said, as though he were watching a linebacker race for a touchdown. Jennifer watched.

'David, I don't think it's going to work. You can't do this kind of thing anyway,' she said finally. 'Hey, you know there's this movie on at the . . .'

GAMES, the monitor lettered.

David said, 'Hot dog!'

The monitor continued.

FALKEN'S MAZE

BLACKJACK
CHECKERS
CHESS
FIGHTER COMBAT
DESERT WARFARE
THEATERWIDE TACTICAL WARFARE.

'Huh?' said David Lightman. 'These aren't . . .'

'Wait a minute,' Jennifer said. 'There's one more.'

GLOBAL THERMONUCLEAR WAR.

'Holy smoke,' said David.

'I guess that's like Missile Command, huh, David?' said Jennifer. 'Maybe we could play?'

Daylight lingered over the suburbs as Jennifer Mack zoomed through the parking lots of Seattle University, David Lightman hanging on for dear life onto the back of her moped.

'So who is this guy again?' Jennifer asked as they negotiated a sidewalk shortcut.

'Uh . . . Jim Sting,' David said, wondering if it had been wise to ask Jennifer to drive him here right away. He'd been so excited, and she had nothing much else to do, so they just jumped on the bike and braved the rush hour to let Jim Sting have a look at the printout. David had ordered the system he'd found to run each of the games, to absolutely no avail. He'd immediately thought of Jim.

'You know all my equipment?' he said, jangled from a recent bump.

'Yeah. You've got scads of it!' said Jennifer, dodging a Farrah Fawcett look-alike coed.

'How'd you think I could afford all that? My parents aren't

exactly rich, and they really don't approve of my hobby.'

'Your obsession, you mean.'

'Yeah, well, whatever.'

'I dunno,' said Jennifer. 'You rob somebody?'

'Uh uh. I got most of it from Jim Sting, real cheap.'

'A computer equipment fence?' Jennifer wondered.

'Naw. He works here at the university's computer facility. Repair shop. He's a real whiz at it. He could do a lot of things with computers – and he does. But what he likes best is building them. He used to be a Phone Phreak. Messed Ma Bell all up, and never got caught.'

'What, with one of those little black boxes?'

'You bet. Jim was the best. Then he just got tired of it. No more challenge, you know?' David gave her some direction, and they putt-putted across a green mall where students lounged or tossed Frisbees.

'How'd you meet him?'

'Classifieds. He had a disk drive I needed up for sale. So I met him and started asking questions, and pretty soon I was spending half my time with him, learning lots. Heck, I must have spent half of last summer in his shop. Worth four years in stupid Humphrey High. Up that hill, Jennifer, then around behind that building.'

Jennifer executed the command like the hotdogger she was. 'Park here.' David indicated a bike stand. 'And lock it. You can't trust university students these days. I think they're all clones of Richard Nixon and Ronald Raygun.'

'Hey! My dad's a Republican!' Jennifer said as they skipped up the steps to the entrance.

David held a glass door open for her. 'So's mine. Q.E.D.'

He led her down a fluorescently lit corridor, past rooms

where students intently ogled monitor screens and diddled on keyboards. Some played games, others seemed to be programming.

'Talk about clones, pal.' She gestured about. 'Meet thy spiritual brethren.'

David attempted a Peter Lorre voice. 'We all landed here from outer space in pods, my dear, and we're taking over you human beings body by body. Soon you too will sit in front of a computer monitor and drool.'

Jennifer laughed. 'Invasion of the Body Hackers.'

'You're remembering the terminology, anyway. Hang a right here.'

The repair shop was at the end of a corridor. Piles of computer equipment, big and small, lay scattered about among soldering irons and miscellaneous other equipment. The place held the stench of burned insulation. From a gutted housing protruded two legs and an oversize rear end.

'Is that your genius?' Jennifer said.

'Yeah. Sting has extra memory-storage capacity in his extremities. Good 48 K, I'd say. Wait here, okay?'

David stepped up to the housing. 'Hey, Cap'n Crunch. I'm from Ma Bell, and boy, is she angry.'

Sting, retracting his head, clunked it against a cabinet. 'Ouch!' he said, crawling out from amid the confusion of circuit boards and wire looms.

'Naw, just his little brother.'

'Lightman!' he smiled, rubbing his head. He was a chunky guy, with a flannel shirt that hung out over faded jeans. He carried himself with an air of arrogance. David always fancied him a renegade truck driver. 'Hey Malvin, don't pull out the Uzi submachine gun, it's just David Lightman.

Haven't see ya for a while, Dave. Fall into that black hole game you were programming?'

Around the other side of the bench strode Malvin, a thin, hyper student type who looked like he had just escaped the robots from Berserk.

'Cap'n, can you take a look at this?' David pulled the folded printout sheet from his pocket.

'Howdy, Lightman,' Malvin said, 'How are the programs byting? What on earth is this?'

He grabbed the printout.

'Wait, I want Jim to see it.'

Malvin's eyes were big in his narrow, angular face. 'Where did you get this?'

'I was trying to break into Protovision. I wanted to get the programs for some new games.'

Sting reached for the paper, but Malvin turned away. 'Wait, I'm not through.'

'Shit you're not through!' Sting grabbed the paper, straightening his smudgy glasses. He scratched his straggly beard. 'Global thermonuclear war. This didn't come from Protovision.'

'I know it doesn't,' Malvin whined. 'Ask him where he got it.'

'I told you,' said David.

Malvin said, 'Must be military. Definitely military.' He looked up and speared Lightman with a suspicious glance. 'Probably classified.'

David said, 'Yeah, I thought about that. But if it's military, why would they have games like blackjack and checkers?'

'Maybe because they're games that teach basic strategy,' Jim Sting suggested.

Malvin noticed Jennifer, who was watching the group from a slight distance. 'Who's that?' he asked, his thin lips twitching a bit.

'She's with me.'

'Why is she standing over there listening?' Malvin wanted to know.

'She's not listening. She gave me a ride over here,' replied David. 'Jennifer. Come on over here. I want you to meet my friends.'

Jennifer stepped up hesitatingly. David made the introductions. Sting and Malvin seemed a bit off-put by the arrival of a female among them. Malvin grinned a lot, and Sting studiously avoided looking at her. It was as though, David thought, the girl held some dark secret about them both.

Jennifer sat in a chair and waited patiently.

'Anyway, Jim, how can I get into this system? These games must be *fabulous*. I wanna *play* stuff like this. I've never seen anything like this.'

Malvin tucked the back of his shirt in. 'And you're not supposed to see stuff like this. Anyway, that system probably has the new date encryption algorithm. You'll never get in.'

David was insistent. 'I don't believe any system is totally secure. I betcha Jim could get in.'

Malvin looked at his colleague. 'Not even Jim, my friend.'

They both looked at the bulky, shaggy man for a moment, Malvin with a kind of challenge, David entreatingly.

Jim scratched a flaky nose. 'No way you can get in the front-line security,' he said finally.

Malvin smirked.

'But,' said Jim, a Cap'n Crunch gleam of malicious glee in his eyes, 'you might look for a back door.'

Malvin's narrow eyes widened considerably. 'I can't believe it. This girl is sitting here, listening, and you're telling Lightman about back doors!'

Sting chuckled. 'Hey, Malvin, relax! Back doors are no secret.' His big stomach quivered with mirth.

'Well, you're giving up tricks that belong to us, anyway,' Malvin said indignantly.

David grabbed onto this. 'What tricks? What's a back door?'

Jim hiked up his trousers the way he always did before he got pedantic, then folded his arms across his chest. 'Well, when I design a system, I always put in a simple password that only I know about. So later, if I want to get back in, I can bypass whatever security they've added on.'

Incredible! Wonderful! thought David. *Of course, it's so obvious, why didn't I think of such a thing!*

'Ah, Jennifer. Could you not touch that?' Malvin said nervously. 'That's a tape drive and I'm having a lot of trouble with that unit.'

'Sorry,' Jennifer said, batting innocent eyes at Malvin.

'So go ahead, man!' David said enthusiastically.

'If you really want to get in, you should probably find out everything you can about the guy who designed the system.'

David was crestfallen. 'How do I even find out who the guy is?'

'Well, ah –' Jim said, pondering the problem.

'Lemme see that paper there, Cap'n,' Malvin said impatiently. 'You guys are so dumb! I don't believe it. I bet I know how to do it. I figured it out.'

Old Malvin was a regular Eddie Haskell, David thought. 'Oh, yeah, Malvin. So how would you do it?'

75

Malvin grinned. 'First game on the list, you dummies. *I'd* go in through Falken's Maze.'

'Falken, huh?'

'Yeah, it's probably the name of the joker who programmed this gaming system.'

'Could be. And maybe he's well known,' Sting said, nodding. 'So what you've gotta do, David, is find out who this Falken fellow is before you can do anything.'

'Huh?'

'Check out the library, man,' Malvin said.

'Yeah. Good idea,' David said.

'But watch yourself, man,' Malvin warned. 'This may just be games, but they probably belong to some powerful game-masters.'

David grinned. 'If I get in, there's no way they're gonna catch me. You know, maybe they'll have some new routines *nobody* knows about. Maybe I can use them in some games of my own devising. Anyway, this should be *neat*.'

'Peachy keen, Lightman,' said Jim Sting. 'Now, if you and your lady friend will excuse me, I have to get back to work.'

On their way out, David turned to Jennifer and said, 'Understand any of that?'

'Not much.' She winked. 'Sounds like you're going to be naughty, though.'

'Naw. This ain't going to hurt anybody,' said David Lightman, a sense of real challenge charging up his mental batteries. 'I'm just going to have some *fun*.'

Chapter Five

Step on a crack, break your mother's back.

Bam, bam, bam. Lower spine . . .

Hah, hah, hah, take that Mother dear, thought Jennifer Mack as she jogged along the sidewalk adjacent to Park Avenue, enjoying a bright spring Sunday afternoon. *That'll teach you to be such a nag!*

Jennifer loped along glumly, singing to herself a variation on Olivia Newton-John's song 'Physical', substituting the word *cynical*.

Bobby Jason had called her up earlier canceling their date tonight. The twerp. 'Not feeling so good, Jenny,' he'd said. 'I think it's that flu going around.' Yeah, sure, and her name was probably Barbara 'Germ' McAllister, the one with the chest so big she couldn't stand up straight. The cow.

Jennifer Mack wore tan shorts, a tank top, Keds shoes, and a pink sweatband, and she knew she didn't look half bad. She enjoyed jogging. Her dad was the fitness freak, and it was he that had encouraged her. She'd started out her adolescence a little on the chubby side, but thanks to this, a little tennis, some skiing in the winter, and aerobics classes at the Y, she kept the weight down without having to give up teen treats like pizza and milkshakes and Cokes and popcorn with lots of butter. No smoking, though – she was too smart for that. Her mom smoked like a fiend, and coughed all the time, too, so Jennifer lived with a good incentive to abstain from peer pressure in that area.

Jennifer Mack considered herself a fairly normal teenager, who got the odd pimple but didn't have acne, who studied harder than she wanted her friends to know, who talked about boys a lot but knew very little about them or the mysterious things they always seemed to be whispering and giggling about. Big deal!

She had an older brother in college, and a brat of a little prepubescent sister who always got into her record collection. She had, in short, the average, *boooooring* American girl's life. Where was the romance? Where was the glamour? Like that Peggy Lee song her mother liked to listen to, 'Is That All There Is?'

Her sneakered feet clopped along the cement. She executed a quick turn. The breeze blew back her hair and was cool on her sweaty face. A man clipping his hedge paused and watched her pass. *Make way for the Foxy Lady*, she thought.

She jogged along another couple of blocks, then suddenly realized she was passing David Lightman's street. He hadn't been in school for two days. Jennifer wondered what he'd been up to. Fooling with that computer of his, no doubt. Although she hadn't mentioned the business with the grades, she had told her mom about the new guy she'd met with the computer obsession. Her mother had shaken her head. 'With your father at that age it was cars. Nowadays, it seems cars are on the way out. Thank goodness your father doesn't have one of those personal computers. I hear it can wreck a marriage.'

78

'Mom,' she had said. 'If David Lightman was as up on cars as he was on computers, he'd be racing the Daytona 500!'

Despite his weirdness, Jennifer kind of liked him. He had a delightful shyness about him, a gentleness that had a definite air of mystery to it. Besides, if he gained a little weight, went out in the sun a little more often, and wore some better clothes, maybe he'd be real cute. Well, close enough for rock 'n' roll anyway. At least he didn't try to paw her and breathe heavy on her like a lot of the jocks she'd gone out with. Sometimes she wondered if they really enjoyed that stuff, or if it was just in their genes. She could almost imagine Mr Ligett lecturing about chromosomes and football in American teen-age males.

Jennifer Mack figured that as long as she was in the area, she'd pay a call on David Lightman. Not that she was really interested in the guy. She was just curious. Besides, now that he'd changed her grade, she had a sort of obligation to him. She had to make sure he was okay. It had nothing to do with her emotions whatsoever.

About fifty yards up Elm was the Lightman residence. She puffed up the walk, pounded on the door.

An unpleasant-looking man with glasses answered as though expecting a pitch for Girl Scout cookies. Jennifer Mack put on her bounciest I'm-your-neighborly-sweet-and-optimistic-virgin voice and asked, 'Hi, is David here?'

The man stared at her.

'You must be Mr Lightman, right?'

'That's correct.'

'I'm Jennifer. David and I have class together.'

Still Mr Lightman stood in the doorway, a look of mild disbelief tinged with embarrassed curiosity colored his face.

Suddenly it registered to Jennifer how she must look in her sweaty jogging outfit. She blushed.

'I've been jogging.'

Mr Lightman coughed and looked away. 'Yes. Glad to see a healthy ... uhm. Yes, David. David is up in his room.' He stepped aside, allowing Jennifer to enter.

'Thanks.'

As she headed for the staircase, Mr Lightman looked on with astonishment, seeing that she knew exactly where to go. 'You've been here before?'

'Oh, yes,' she said mischievously, 'David is such a wonderful boy.'

'You've been to his room?'

'Uh huh.'

'What's it like in there?'

She sighed and turned her eyes heavenward. 'Delightful.'

Mr Lightman, perplexed, straightened out the newspaper in his hand. 'You ought to take him out running. He never gets any exercise.'

'I promise I'll exercise him for you, Mr Lightman,' she said cheerily, giving him a wave as her smooth legs carried her up past his astonished eyes.

A knock on his door brought out a grumpy 'Yeah?'

'It's me,' she said. 'Jennifer.'

'Jennifer?' There was the sound of footsteps coming toward the door. It clicked open. David Lightman looked out like some kind of mole peering from its burrow. 'Hey. Hi. Come on in.'

She stepped into the room. 'Yow,' she said. 'It looks like a bomb hit.' The normally cluttered room was now a total wreck. Papers, magazines, and reams of printouts were spread everywhere, to say nothing of dirty laundry, Coke cans, Frito packages, and unidentified grounded objects. His equipment was in full swing, busy lights on disk drives blipping, monitors displaying that list of games that had him in such a tizzy, another TV set on, hooked to a video cassette recorder. The place had the compound odor of a locker room in a library.

'I've been preoccupied,' David said, settling down in front of his keyboard.

'I'll say. Where have you been, anyway?'

David was suddenly concentrating on the monitor display. 'What?' he asked absently.

The jerk hadn't even noticed her skimpy attire. What was wrong with him, anyway? His father had sure noticed.

A little peeved, Jennifer said, 'I haven't seen you around.'

'Yeah, well ... Oh. Sorry.' He got up and hastily moved some books off the bed so that she could sit.

As Jennifer did so, she asked, 'Just what *is* all this stuff, David?'

'I went to the library,' David said.

'No *kidding*!'

'I'm trying to find out more about the guy who made these programs so I can maybe figure out his private password.'

'Oh yeah?'

'Yeah.' David's eyes lit up. 'Jennifer ... it was simple. I just looked up the name "Falken" in the huge card catalogue of the science library at the university.' He pulled out a large yellow pad filled with notes. 'His name is Stephen W. Falken, and the first thing I came across was a listing for *Falken's Maze – Teaching a Machine to Think*. So I tried it on the computer. Didn't work. So I got all of the stuff he published out ... and I found out that Falken died in 1973. Well, I've been playing around ever since on lots of stuff and –'

'Hey. Wait a minute. Just who *is* this fellow Falken, anyway. Did you find that out?'

'Oh, yeah! He was English. Worked for the U.S. Department of Defense a whole lot.'

'You know, David. You're absolutely bananas. Just tell me what's so special about playing games with some machine that you knock yourself out like this. It's ridiculous.'

'It's not just some machine, Jennifer, can't you understand? I'm going to be able to learn a lot if I can get in! Here. You wanted to know about Falken.' He grabbed up a half-inch videotape cassette and stuck it into his VCR. 'Take a look at this!' He hit the 'play' button.

The TV showed images of a bunch of games, with a voice-over talking about strategy and machines. It was black and white – old. Then a guy appeared.

'That's Falken,' David said. 'He's showing off a prototype of his computer. He was really into games as well as computers. He programmed them to play all kinds of games – chess, checkers.'

'Well, doesn't everybody do that now?' Jennifer said.

'No, no,' David objected. 'What he did that was so great was he designed the computers to learn from their mistakes so they got better the next game. The system really learns how to learn. It teaches itself. Now, if I could just figure out the password, I could play the computer. I could learn so much. I could apply this to new programs. I could . . .'

'You know, he's really *cute*,' Jennifer said, watching TV. 'Too bad he's dead. You could just call him up. He must have died very young.'

'Naw. He was pretty old I think,' David said. 'Forty-one or something.'

'That old!'

'Yeah. I found his obituary.' David handed her a printout.

The TV showed a picture of a three-year-old boy playing at the computer. A closer look revealed that he was playing tic-tac-toe.

'That's his little boy,' David said.

Jennifer perused the obit. 'You know, this is really sad. It says the son and his mother were killed in some car wreck.'

'Yep.'

'Falken died when he was forty-one. You know, I just remember, *my* dad is forty-five. I remember he was really sick once. And we all thought he was going to –'

David stood bolt upright, a look on his face like he'd been hit by a jolt of electricity. 'What's his name?' he demanded.

'My *dad*?'

'No, Falken's son. What was his name?'

Jennifer looked at the printout again. 'It says here "Joshua".'

David's eyes sparkled. 'I'm going to give it a try.'

'Give what a try?'

'For his own private password, he probably picked out something from his personal life ... something nobody else would even think about. Maybe it was Joshua, his son, who played with computers too!'

David sat down at the keyboard and typed in JOSHUA as the password.

YOU HAVE BEEN DISCONNECTED, said the monitor.

'It shouldn't be *that* simple, David,' Jennifer said. 'I have an idea.'

David slumped in his chair, despondent. 'Oh, yeah, sure. Jennifer Mack, the computer genius. I've been banging my head against the keyboard for a couple of days, and you think you can come up with an answer in a couple of minutes.'

'Hey, give me a break!' said Jennifer, quite annoyed. 'It'll just take you a couple of seconds to try this.'

'Okay. What is it?' David said wearily.

'Maybe it's more than just "Joshua",' she suggested, looking down at the obituary. 'Like, maybe it was the name of his wife and his son.'

'Naw, it would be just one name. I'll try his wife. What was her name?'

'Margaret,' Jennifer answered.

It didn't work.

'Wait a minute,' Jennifer said, getting into the spirit of the hunt. 'It says that Joshua was five years old when he died. Maybe you should tag a 5 at the end of Joshua!'

David shrugged. 'It's sure worth a try.'

Jennifer stood to watch him as he typed in: JOSHUA 5.

The monitor did not disconnect.

Suddenly letters and numbers totally incomprehensible to Jennifer began to pour across the monitor screen.

'Wow!' said David.

'What's going on?'

'We've *got* something,' David said jubilantly, giving her a broad smile. A little shiver of excitement coursed up Jennifer's back.

Abruptly the monitor went black.

'Uh uh,' said Jennifer.

'No, wait,'

Letters coursed across the screen: GREETINGS, PROFESSOR FALKEN.

'We *are* in!' said David, exultant. 'It thinks I'm Falken!' David quickly typed in: HELLO.

84

The TV set responded with: HOW ARE YOU FEELING TODAY?

Jennifer was astonished. 'Why does it ask you *that*?'

'It'll ask you whatever it's programmed to ask you,' David replied. 'Want to hear it talk?'

'Talk? You mean like – uh – verbalize?'

'Yep!' David tapped a small box replete with switches and knobs. 'This is a voice synthesizer. I just turn it on ...' Click. 'And it interprets the words syllable by syllable. Listen. I'm going to ask how it feels.'

David typed in, I'M FINE. HOW ARE YOU?

The machine responded with letters across the screen. And a voice interpreted those letters simultaneously in a nasal monotone.

'Ex-cel-lent,' it said. 'It's been a long time. Can you explain the removal of your user account number on June 23, 1973?'

David typed in: PEOPLE SOMETIMES MAKE MIS-TAKES.

The machine said, 'Yes, they do.'

YES THEY DO lingered on the screen.

Jennifer said, 'I don't understand.'

'It's not a real voice,' David explained. 'This box just translates the signal from the sound.'

The machine said, 'Shall we play a game?'

SHALL WE PLAY A GAME? echoed the letters on the screen.

'It's almost ...' said Jennifer, absolutely fascinated. 'Almost as though it *misses* Falken.'

David nodded slowly. 'Yeah! Weird, isn't it?'

A strange smile crept over David's face. Jennifer didn't like that smile very much, but it intrigued her. It spoke of victory – but it also spoke of mischief.

David typed in: HOW ABOUT THERMONUCLEAR WAR?

'Would you prefer a good game of chess?' the machine said flatly.

LATER, David typed. LET'S PLAY GLOBAL THERMONUCLEAR WAR.

'Fine,' the machine responded. 'What side do you want?'

'All *right*!' said David. 'This should be a blast!'

I'LL BE THE RUSSIANS, he typed.

'List primary targets,' the machine requested.

David turned to Jennifer. 'What a game! What do you want to nuke first?'

Jennifer said, 'Las Vegas. My dad lost a bunch of money there once.'

'Okay! Las Vegas gets it *ker-blam*! Let's see what else. Definitely Seattle.'

'Yuck, yes! I'm really sick of Seattle,' Jennifer agreed.

They both giggled.

David Lightman then typed out a number of other cities.

'Thank you,' the machine said.

'What next? Do we get to watch?'

'I dunno.'

'Game commencing,' the computer said.

Then the screen went blank.

'Hey, did something go wrong?' Jennifer said.

'I don't know.'

'Gee, it's a slow game.'

'Some of these strategy games take a while.'

Suddenly data began filling the screen. 'Geez,' said David, 'I forgot to turn on my disk drive to save all this.' He quickly remedied the situation. 'Here we go, Jennifer. Are you ready for World War III, Comrade Mack?'

'*Da*, Comrade,' Jennifer said, saluting. 'Nuke those decadent imperialists!'

They both laughed uproariously.

In the Crystal Palace, the cavernous womb carrying its hunkering, glittery machines of death, it was business as usual. The place had a weird feeling, half library, half tomb. Technicians spoke in muted voices or not at all as they served their tours of duties, swiveling in their chairs, taking readings, monitoring surface activity in the Soviet Union, or the monsoon sweeping toward Borneo. Display technicians peered into their scopes, holding the translated messages of thousands of radar and sonar tracking devices. In darker parts of the amphitheater, the equipment cast an eerie glow upon their faces, while communication folk murmured into headsets or phones. Some seventy military personnel manned their posts now, highly qualified experts all, while the great electronic maps hung aloft like expectant prophecies.

Above them, the scoreboard for the dreaded but anticipated future game indicated the current defense condition.

DEFCON 5

DEFCON 5 meant peacetime. DEFCON 1 meant total war; 4, 3, and 2 were all the juicy parts in between.

General Jack Berringer sat in his shirt sleeves in the command balcony, opposite the big screens, wondering where his coffee was. General Jack Berringer was not in a particularly good mood.

His son, Jimmy, was not in the military. In fact, his son, Jimmy, was a deadbeat, studying for some obscure English degree in some obscure college in northern California, and Dad paid for it. *Where was the draft now that* I *need it* was a major preoccupation for the general. His daughters were married off and having grandchildren, as dutiful girls should, but his only son defied his father by having the nerve not to enlist. Mrs Berringer, beaming, had just shown him a letter that morning from Jimmy, commenting on how wonderful the twenty-five-year-old was doing and how well the letter was written. General Berringer had opined that he'd rather see the wimp wielding an M-16 in the fields of honor than a pen in the prissy halls of academia. That had touched off a brief spat between the general and the Mrs, fully resembling those between General Halftrack of *Beetle Bailey* and *his* wife. General Berringer hated that comic. He hated *Doonesbury*, too, and was damned glad it was out of his paper, if only for a while. Where had all the good comics gone, like *Li'l Abner* and *Terry and the Pirates*?

General Jack Berringer was also teed off that Dr John McKittrick had done so damned well on his trip to Washington last year. He'd gotten his wishes, the turkey. His stupid WOPR was neck-deep in it all now, and McKittrick was prancing around with a big irritating grin all over his face. 'I get a dozen medals in Korea and 'Nam, and this is the thanks I get,' he murmured to himself.

'Where's Sergeant Reilly?' he asked, of no one in particular. 'Where's my coffee?'

He had a headache coming on, and he needed the coffee to wash enough aspirin down to keep him going.

Colonel Conley, his chief communications officer, was

beside him, fiddling with his gear. 'You asked for cream, Jack. Maybe they're out of cream.'

'Out of cream! Not damned likely,' General Berringer said. 'I've got enough coffee in these digs to ride out a nuclear holocaust, and you can bet I have enough cream to drink it with. You know I need the cream, Al. Need it for my damned ulcer.' He glowered over toward the main WOPR terminal, manned by Major Frederick Lem. 'An ulcer getting worse, by the way, because of that damned machine McKittrick has got messing up our lives now.'

'Jack, if you're having trouble with an ulcer, you should be drinking Maalox, not coffee.'

General Jack Berringer grumbled. He looked up to see his staff sergeant approaching, holding a steaming cup.

'About time,' the general said, taking the coffee. 'Hey! Where's the cream?'

The staff sergeant smiled and produced four half 'n' half mini-containers from his pocket. 'Thought you'd like to dump them in yourself, sir.'

Meanwhile, Radar Analyst Tyson Adler took a careful sip of hot herbal tea tasting of almonds. You weren't supposed to drink anything near your console, and with good reason. A container of liquid, spilled in just the right spot, could short out a whole board. But Adler's throat was killing him. He'd been out all last night with a date, dancing, and the exertion had somehow brought on a cold. Adler supposed they shouldn't have gone skipping through rain puddles. Oh well, he would survive.

He carefully put a lid back on the tea container, then set it down by his chair. The very moment his face was turned from his radar scope, an electronic blip appeared over the horizon.

Two more.

Then a whole flock of blips moved in a trajectory toward the western United States.

Radar Analyst Adler sighed as he rose up to peer back into his electronic crystal ball. Julie was supposed to be cooking spaghetti for him tonight, and she was not the best cook in the world and . . .

Wait a minute!

He stared at the blips on the scope for a split second, then grabbed his phone.

'I have seven . . .' he said, 'correction, eight Red Birds at two degrees past apogee, projected target areas . . . NORAD regions two-five and two-six.'

In a matter of moments a wailing signal commenced, and heads popped up along the rows of consoles like students awakened from their afternoon naps.

Radar Analyst Adler's message caught Captain Kent Newt daydreaming. He quickly pulled himself from his reverie, adjusted his monitor, and punched up the direct line to the Alaskan NORAD base.

'Cobra Dane,' he said, heart beginning to race. 'We have a Soviet missile warning. Check for malfunction and report confidence . . .'

The siren caught Airman Maggie Fields halfway to the ladies' room. In nothing like military fashion, she about-faced and rushed at breakneck speed back to her chair, scrambling to put on her headset, thinking, *Talk about bad timing!*

'All stations,' she said tersely, eyeing her terminal. 'This is Crystal Palace, initiation and emergency conference.'

Beside her Lieutenant Morgan hopped hastily into his

chair and slipped on his headset. He had been down the aisle, talking to that redhead.

Too busy to be frightened, Radar Analyst Adler was still reporting what his scope showed him. '... Nineteen degrees past apogee with eighteen possible targets in track. Estimate re-entry at twenty-three, nineteen, Zulu.'

General Jack Berringer tried to wipe up the coffee he'd spilled on his pants.

'Sir,' Colonel Conley said, 'we have a radar tracking of eight inbound Soviet I CBMs already over the pole.' Conley's slightly protuberant eyes seemed a bit glazed with shock, but his mouth indicated that he was carrying out his duties. He checked some hastily scribbled notes.

'Estimated impact ... twelve ... make that eleven minutes. Confirmed target area: western United States.'

General Berringer was stunned for a split second. Then his head jerked up to the central screen, representing North America and its surrounding seas. That very instant eight blips appeared on the screen headed for the continent.

'Why didn't we get a launch detection from the spy satellites?' General Berringer demanded.

Sweat had broken out on Conley's brow, just below the hairline. 'I'm not sure, sir. We're checking for DSP malfunction.' Conley turned back to his communications board, feverishly going back to work.

General Berringer thought, *And we were just getting the talks set up. Never did trust that Andropov character.*

Radar Analyst Adler felt like he was about to throw up. The graphics in his screen told the dreadful story as clear as day. Swallowing, taking a deep breath, he adjusted the skewed mouthpiece of his headset and reported what he saw.

'BMEWS has continuous radar tracking on inbounds ... confidence is high ... I repeat, confidence is high.'

I love ya, Mom, thought Adler.

Close to a thousand miles away, two teen-agers sat amid a scatter of computer equipment, staring in fascination at the screen of a nineteen-inch Sylvania TV set. Across that screen flowed a fleeting jumble of printouts that looked to Jennifer Mack something like Egyptian hieroglyphics on fast forward. The boy's face registered unadulterated glee as he answered any queries from the machine, typing rapidly into the terminal, then peering up to see what the results were.

'What does all that mean?' Jennifer wished to know.

David Lightman smiled. 'I don't know, but it sure is great!'

The symbols flitted across the screen like electronic phantoms chasing one another toward doomsday, then back to the WOPR computer deep in Cheyenne Mountain, quite close to the Crystal Palace's command balcony, where Lieutenant Harlan Dougherty, a lanky communications aide, leaned over a printer.

Dougherty ripped out a printout and barked its contents over to General Jack Berringer, whose nails were digging holes into the pads of his chair. '... The President is in his limousine, they are diverting to Andrews ... The Vice-President is out of position ... The Chairman of the Joint Chiefs is –'

Colonel Conley jerked his head up from the communications board, cutting into Dougherty's report.

'Missile warning reports no malfunction. Confidence remains high,' he said, suddenly aware of a slight dizziness. He'd always wondered what it would be like when this business wasn't just a drill or a test. Conley knew now, and he wondered if, despite the training, despite his professionalism, he was going to make it.

'Take us to DEFCON 3,' General Jack Berringer ordered. 'Get on to SAC. Have them flush out the bombers.'

Hands flew, obeying his orders. Berringer stared up to the electronic scoreboard above, which still read DEFCON 5. In a blink of an eye it changed to DEFCON 3. *So far, so good,* thought Berringer.

Captain Kent Newt, in the communications module, noticed the sign change, noticed on the edge of his vision the technicians and officers scurrying about, noticed the chatter of voices, the increased blinking of lights. But his mind was fixed on the duty just assigned him. He pushed the button that would complete the code already fed into the phone, then spoke into his headset.

'SAC, this is Crystal Palace,' he said. 'C-in-C NORAD declares DEFCON 3. Scramble all alert aircraft. I repeat, scramble all alert aircraft.'

Radar Analyst Adler, on the floor below, still gazed into his screen, which mirrored exactly what was happening on the big board above. The eight missiles headed for North America split off into multiple warheads.

'Inbounds presently MIRVing,' reported Radar Analyst Adler. 'We now have approximately twenty-four possible targets in track.'

Lieutenant Dougherty heard that report and glanced at a readout screen. 'Sir,' he said to General Berringer, 'new time to impact, eight minutes!'

Up in the command balcony, Colonel Conley handed a phone to General Berringer. 'Sir,' he said tersely, 'SAC is launching the bombers ... General Powers is on the line.'

'Berringer here,' said the general into the phone.

'What have you guys been doing?' General Powers virtually screamed over the line. 'Standing around with your fingers in your ears?'

'God damn it,' Berringer said defensively, 'we never *got* a launch detection from the satellites. Radar picked 'em up already out of the atmosphere, and that's the first thing we heard.'

'Yeah, well if this is the real thing, we're going to need more than bombers. And if it is, Berringer ...' There was a pause from Powers, a lightening of the tone. 'I'll see you in hell, okay?'

'Yeah, Bill.' Berringer hung up, then turned to the board. It was really happening. Unless something changed radically, it was the beginning of the Big Three. When you had a job like Berringer's, you thought about that sort of thing all the time. He sighed. *It's almost a relief,* he thought. But then he thought about his grandchildren and his wife, and even his irritating son studying English in some dandified, prissy college, and suddenly war wasn't just a job, even to him.

Berringer turned to Conley. 'You better have the ICBMs warm up in their bullpens. Get 'em ready to fly.'

Berringer looked back up at the blips blinking on the board, drawing steadily closer to the United States. Each was a missile, screaming through the atmosphere, carrying megatons of nuclear destruction, bearing screeching wind and searing fire that would tear apart cities and millions of human lives in just a few heartbeats of time.

The Grim Reaper could have a real big day ahead of him, Berringer thought.

'Sir?' Berringer suddenly realized that an aide was standing next to him, holding a yellow phone. Berringer took it. The people in the command balcony turned toward him, knowing what that yellow phone meant.

The most dreaded of all decisions was about to be made.

'You know,' said David Lightman to Jennifer Mack, looking up from the monitor with its parade of letters and symbols, 'I think I'm getting the hang of this thing. I wish it had more graphics, though. When I do my own version, I'm definitely going to have to plot out some jim-dandy graphics!'

'And sounds?' Jennifer said. 'Can you make sounds, like on the arcade machines?'

'Oh, sure. Real roaring noises, explosions . . . *ka-boom! Kerblam!*'

'And screams with that voice synthesizer?' Jennifer asked, a morbid smile on her face.

'Not with the synthesizer. You ever heard a monotone scream?' He turned his attention back to the monitor, where new lettering was displayed, followed by a question mark.

'Comrade Mack,' he said, in a poor attempt at a Russian accent, 'Comrade Joshua wishes to know if we care to deploy submarine forces.'

Jennifer Mack giggled. 'Sure! Give 'em the works.'

'*Da*, Comrade, comink up!'

He was about to type in the appropriate orders, when a loud crash sounded from the backyard, followed by a series of frenzied barks.

'Uh oh,' said David. 'The American K-9 corps have been sent to attack us, Comrade Mack. Call the Kremlin! Call the KGB!'

'David!' cried a voice. 'David!'

'Comrade Lightman, the Americans are bringing out their secret weapon!'

They both were about to go into hysterics, but David managed to make it to the window and looked down through the screen. There he was, Commander Lard himself, standing by two knocked-over garbage cans, staring up with an indignant expression on his kisser. Litter lay strewn all about him.

'David,' he yelled up, 'I've told you you've got to fasten down the lids. Look at this mess!'

'I'll be down in a few minutes, Dad,' David said.

'Not in a few minutes!' Mr Lightman yelled. 'Now! You hear me? I want this picked up *right now*! Understand?'

His mother walked out and looked at the mess, then glanced up at David, speaking in a kinder tone of voice. 'Honey, will you come down here and do what your father says?'

David hopped off the bed, knocking off a few books in the process.

'The final ultimatum, Comrade?' Jennifer asked, looking up with an understanding expression.

'Yeah. The damned spoilsports. Just when the game was getting really good!' He went over to the keyboard and stared at it with regret.

'Cripes,' he said, turning off the whole system.

On the big central map of North America in NORAD's Crystal Palace, everything began to blink.

Suddenly all the boards went blank. The wailing signal, musical accompaniment to the crisis, ceased.

Radar Analyst Adler said, 'Huh?'

Captain Newt said, 'What the hell?'

Colonel Conley fumbled with his controls.

Then the boards slowly came back on.

None of them showed even a trace of any approaching Russian missiles.

Colonel Conley listened for a moment to his earpiece, then looked over to where General Berringer stood, growing armpit stains showing on his light blue shirt.

'General, BMEWS and Cobra Dane now report negative confirmation on all inbound tracking.'

The message took a moment to register with Berringer. Hope flooded through him. 'Get SAC,' he ordered. 'Tell them to hold steady!'

To one side of his vision he saw a sweatered man rushing desperately onto the floor of the Crystal Palace, waving his arms frantically to attract attention.

Paul Richter yelled as loud as he could and still maintain coherence. 'Stop it! *Stop!*' The faces of technicians swiveled his way, astonished. 'It's a simulation,' he cried. 'There's an attack simulation running!'

As soon as he had realized what was happening, Paul Richter had raced out of the WOPR room. *I have to get to the command balcony before the missiles are launched*, he thought, dodging an empty chair, reaching the bottom of the steps.

General Berringer, in the command balcony, was nonplussed. 'What's he saying?' he asked of anyone within earshot.

A technician got in the way. Richter shoved him aside, and pounded up the steps. He almost threw himself into the command balcony, saying breathlessly, 'We're *not* being attacked!' He drew in a difficult breath. He was terribly out of shape for this kind of thing. 'It's a simulation! For God's sake, don't –'

Berringer was standing, his face still red. 'What the hell is going on here?' he demanded. 'You know we don't allow running here. Someone could get *hurt*!'

Richter said breathlessly, 'Sorry sir. We're not really certain how, but someone on the outside fed an attack simulation into the main system.'

Pat Healy was on Richter's heels. In her hands was a computer printout. She handed it to Richter.

McKittrick and his wonderful machines, Berringer thought. *And the jerk isn't even here to see this!*

Berringer said, 'Conley, get us off full alert and hold at DEFCON 4 until we find out exactly what is going on . . .'

Richter looked up from the printout and turned angrily to Pat Healy. 'I didn't tell you to cut the line. Did I tell you to cut the line? You've *cut* the line!' He looked up with a frightened expression at General Berringer. 'Sir, they shut down before we could complete our trace.'

Pat Healy maintained her composure. 'We did locate the general area where the transmission originated.'

'Where?' Berringer demanded.

'Seattle, Washington, sir.'

Chapter Six

The sun looked like a molten coin slipping into an arcade machine slot on the horizon. A pleasant spring breeze stirred the green leaves of the tree bordering David Lightman's street as the teen-ager almost skipped home, Windbreaker aflap, his head thrown back, trying to whistle 'Pac-Man Fever'. Part of the road had just been resurfaced, and the scent of tar hung in the air.

God, he was in a good mood! It had been a *great* Monday. Classes had gone very fast. Jennifer Mack had been quite friendly, in a casual kind of way. Heck, maybe he'd even ask her out to fool around at the arcade sometime – teach her everything he knew about Joust. But that could wait. Jennifer was okay, but after all, first things first.

Waiting for him at home was the disk containing the complete record of the game he'd played with Joshua yesterday. A lot of work there, figuring stuff out, but what a *slew* of information!

What do you know, he thought as he jounced merrily up the sidewalk to his home, noticing that Mom's flowers had bloomed prettily and that their perfume hung in the air along with the odor of new-mown grass from next door. *The folks are home tonight!*

He pulled open the door. His face sported a big, happy grin. The TV set droned in the den. David could see his father's legs and shoes sticking out from his favorite overstuffed chair.

'Hi, Dad,' David called out cheerfully, poking his head into the dark room.

His father grunted and changed the channel.

David shrugged. He hopped up the stairs.

'David!' his mother shouted from below. David froze. There was always something about the way she said his name – probably programmed into him from his childhood – that switched him into instant tension mode. He turned around and headed back down the steps. What was up now, he wondered, bouncing down mopily.

'What did I do?' His mother's voice had been very stern, and she looked very businesslike now as she strode from the kitchen wearing her real estate lipstick and eye shadow. In her right hand was a white card.

'Plenty, mister,' she said, thrusting out the paper. Lightning quick, her expression changed. She smiled! 'You just passed all your classes for the semester. Congratulations, dear!'

David glanced at the paper. Sure enough, all his diddling with the school computer had borne fruit. He shrugged, and his mother gave him a hug.

'Show this to your father *immediately*. I told him you could do it.' She glanced toward the den. 'Honey!' Grabbing his arm, his mother marched him forward.

Oh, please, thought David. He would really much rather get going on the analysis of his game with Joshua.

As they traipsed in, the theme music from the CBS news was finishing. Yep, there was Dan Rather in his ratings-gathering sweater, looking professionally grim as he rattled off the top story of the day. 'For three and half minutes yesterday evening, the defense forces of the United States went on a full-scale nuclear alert.'

'Harold, just take a look at this!' Mrs Lightman said, thrusting the card in Mr Lightman's face.

'Hey, I'm *trying* to watch the news. Didn't you hear?' Mr Lightman said, scrunching around so that he could see the picture tube. 'We had a real crisis today.'

'The belief,' the announcer said, 'was that the Soviet Union had launched a surprise missile attack.'

Huh? thought David suddenly, paying close attention. As he listened, realization crept over him. Disbelief slowly turned into a terrible, paralyzing horror.

'Good heavens,' said Mrs Lightman.

Rather continued. 'A Pentagon spokesman places blame for the error on a computer malfunction, insisting that the problem had been corrected. More on the story from Ike Pappas.'

Mr Lightman's eyes were wide. 'What was I telling you, dear. We're getting closer to the final days than ever! That Pat Robertson on the 700 Club sure knows what he's talking about! David. Are you paying attention?'

David Lightman was indeed paying attention.

The machine had said it was just a game, he thought. Just a game!

'Excuse me,' he said, and ran up to his room, where he turned on the television to watch the rest of the report. A spokesman for the Defense Department was on the screen, explaining that at no time was there any danger – that this was a million-to-one possibility and that it would never, repeat *never*, happen again.

The phone rang.

David jumped. Nervously he went over and picked it up. 'Hello?'

Immediately he recognized Jennifer Mack's voice. 'David. Are you watching TV?'

'The news – uh . . . yeah.'

Jennifer was excited. 'Is that us? Did *we* do that?'

And the realization hit David Lightman finally and totally. His own little world of fun and games had suddenly expanded into a larger, much scarier arena. 'It must be,' he said. 'Oh, wow, I'm really in trouble now. Jennifer, what am I gonna do . . . they're gonna get us.'

Silence from the other end for a moment. 'What do you mean us, white man?' Jennifer said. Then she laughed. 'Hey! Calm down. If they're so smart, they'd have already found you. I mean, it has been a day. Right?'

David wasn't so sure. The U.S. military was a giant, and giants moved slowly. 'Yeah . . . I guess . . .'

'Hey, cool off!' Jennifer said casually. 'Just don't call that number again. Throw it away!'

An inkling of hope surfaced in David's mind. 'You know . . . there is the possibility that I didn't . . . that's right, we had to shut down early and . . . They didn't trace the call!'

'Sure! So just act *normal*. You'll be okay. Don't worry.'

'Yeah. Thanks, Jennifer. You've made me feel a lot better.'

'Oh my God,' she said. 'It's just unbelievable. You think I could just tell Marci?'

David almost had a heart attack. 'No! Jennifer, please.'

'Okay, okay,' she said, clearly disappointed and obviously not fully realizing all the implications. 'I'll talk to you tomorrow at school.'

'Right. 'Bye.'

He hung up the phone and fell onto his bed, hiding his head underneath the pillow, trying to get himself together. *My God*, he thought. *If Ralph hadn't turned over that trash can ... if my dad hadn't demanded that I come down immediately ... if ... if ... if ...*

The world had been saved by a *dog*!

Evidence, David Lightman thought. There was still evidence! He shot up from his bed, panicked. My God, the evidence of his crime surrounded him. Books, magazines, government-published pamphlets of essays and reports littered the place. Printouts were strewn like the aftermath of a Thanksgiving Day parade. From his bookshelf hung a picture of Falken he had photocopied from an old magazine.

David Lightman stared at it for a moment.

Stephen Falken was a thin-faced, delicate-looking sort of fellow, English of hair and mouth, with a look in his eye that stared into lands where David Lightman wished to go. A long, sensitive finger was placed on his temple as though to say, 'This, my friends' – in a very proper British accent, of course – 'is the ultimate computer.'

What a genius the man had been, venturing into marvelous worlds decades before anyone else. Falken would have understood. Falken had known what drove David Lightman – the fascination with such intricate toys, these fusions of metal and glass and plastic and energy, slaves to the magical chants of algorithms. No one else understood – not his parents, nor Jennifer, nor even Jim Sting – what the step-by-step mastery of these machines meant to David. In their world was reason, justice, fairness, order. If you worked hard enough, *you understood* ... not like life. There were rewards for accomplishment ... not like normal life. Mastering programming was like nothing David Lightman had ever known before.

David touched the picture with regret. 'I only ...' he said softly. 'I guess I just wanted to get to know you better,' he told the dead man in the picture.

Then he tore it from its thumbtack and threw it in his overflowing trash basket.

The stacks of books were by the door, ready to be carted out, when David's phone rang.

Was that Jennifer again? She was the only one who had his secret number. The thing was an extension of the Lightman residence phone not registered with Ma Bell. With the help of Jim Sting, David had fixed it up so that he had direct access to the phone company's computer – including free toll calls.

Hesitantly, he picked the phone up.

'Jenn –?'

A high-pitched computer tone hummed. Hmmm. Maybe another hacker had found him. This could take his mind off this awful business.

He slipped the receiver into the modem, turned on his system, and went back to work.

'Greetings, Professor Falken,' the voice synthesizer said.

David froze. He spun around. On the screen were the words GREETINGS, PROFESSOR FALKEN.

He walked to the console and sat. 'Oh God.' Almost of their own volition, his hands rose up and typed in an answer: I AM NOT FALKEN. FALKEN IS DEAD.

The synthesizer said, 'I am sorry to hear that, Professor.

Yesterday's game was interrupted. Although primary goal was not achieved, solution is near.'

On the monitor the words and numbers flitted:

GAME TIME ELAPSED: 26 HRS. 12 MINS. 14 SECS.

ESTIMATED TIME REMAINING: 52 HRS. 17 MINS. 48 SECS.

David's heart seemed to stop. Oh, no. It wasn't over yet! The monitor continued:

...ALTHOUGH PRIMARY GOAL NOT ACHIEVED...

David hit the 'break' button, and typed in: WHAT WAS THE PRIMARY GOAL?

The monitor supplied the answer instantly:

TO WIN THE GAME.

David ripped the receiver from the modem and slammed it down onto the phone cradle. He suddenly realized that his hands were trembling. Quickly he went back to work wiping out the evidence in his room.

The phone rang several more times that night. David Lightman eventually had to disconnect it.

He had a hard time sleeping when he finally went to bed.

That night he dreamed he was Slim Pickens, riding a nuclear bomb shaped like an arcade game down to oblivion.

Chapter Seven

'What's up, Lightman?' asked the black guy behind the 7-Eleven counter. 'You playin' hooky again or somethin'? It's almost ten, man.' The clerk rang up the prices of David's blueberry muffin and carton of milk on his cash register. 'Don't suppose you got time to give me a go on one of them machines, do ya?' The clerk nodded his head at a couple of electronics games in the corner of the store. 'I'm gettin' pretty good on 'em all, what with the nightshift hours I been doin'.'

'Overslept,' David said, handing over a crumpled dollar bill and some change. 'Gotta get to school, Chauncey. Thanks anyway.'

'You know, you got yourself a mean rep for them games. Maybe you oughta enter one of them competitions, win some bread.' Chauncey slipped the money into the cash drawer, then picked up a cigarette and took a drag. 'Guy come in this mornin', askin' 'bout you – said he heard you were a damn fine player. Watcha think? Think he come to challenge you?' Chauncey scratched his beard. 'Well, if so, I'm laying my bread on you, brother.'

David Lightman stopped unwrapping the muffin. The thick stench of newly brewed coffee and the cigarette smoke suddenly made his stomach turn. 'There was a guy asking about me?'

'Yeah! You gettin' famous! Now then, how about you playing me a game of Donkey Kong. I'll beat you bad!'

'What did he look like?'

Chauncey shrugged. 'Hell, I dunno. Young guy. I told him you should be in school now, but you ain't, are you? Hey, where are you going? I got the quarters, man!'

David Lightman slammed through the glass doors and ran through the parking lot. On the sidewalk he slowed down. *Wait a minute*, he told himself. *You're getting paranoid, Lightman. You are well known for being great on video games, and your reputation has been spreading, so maybe the guy asking about you was legit. You gotta take it easy*, he told himself, *or you're going to be a walking bundle of nerves all your life!*

On the road a green van passed him. Up ahead a pair of burly joggers were trotting his way.

Yeah, you gotta get a grip on yourself, or you're going to get no sleep, and you're going to think that every solitary jogger heading your way is packing heat!

He laughed at the notion, and strode along with renewed self-confidence. Like Jennifer said, if they didn't have him now, they probably wouldn't get him. In a few days it would be all over and forgotten. Yes, he'd learned his lesson, all right. No more snooping into places he shouldn't go.

David Lightman considered himself a reformed character.

The joggers were nearer. He moved onto the grass to let them pass – they were a hell of a lot bigger than he, and they didn't look particularly happy.

Instead of passing, however, the joggers trounced onto the grass, too, each grabbing an arm. 'Lightman!' one said, with

107

a look of intense satisfaction. David was hurled onto the grass. Before he knew what was happening, one of the guys was forcing his mouth open and staring into it. 'Don't see any cyanide devices,' he said.

The other had his knee pinning David to the ground. 'You little twerp,' the guy said.

'Hey, get offa me!' David screamed. 'Help! Police!'

The van had returned and stopped by the curb. A crewcut man in a suit and tie was walking toward them. He pulled out a wallet and showed David a badge. 'We're FBI, Lightman. Will that do?'

The joggers emptied his pockets, then handcuffed him. 'Get him in the van,' the man in the suit said. 'We've got a few people who want to talk to you, Mr Lightman.'

David Lightman was hustled into the green van, stunned, bruised, and scared out of his mind.

When the world came to the verge of World War III, John McKittrick had been visiting his mother-in-law.

Now, on the afternoon of the day after the screw-up with his machines, he was back in the Crystal Palace.

'Why wasn't I called immediately, Pat?' he demanded upon arriving at the facility. He and his wife and kids had driven back from Denver early that morning. 'It's my very own responsibility.'

'Richter and I thought we had it all under control, John,' said Pat. 'We thought ...'

'Pat, it's me that gets blamed!' McKittrick said. 'I've got an immediate order to report to General Berringer.' He threw the memo down on his desk. And he'd been feeling so good about everything. The trip to Denver would appease his wife long enough so that he could spend a few late evenings with Pat ... the evacuation of missile commanders was going as planned. Everything had seemed rosy – until this business. 'Well, I guess I'd better face up to it right away.' He stood and put his arms around her. 'I guess, though, that this means there are going to be some evenings when we really *have* to work late.'

'Alas,' she said, kissing him gently.

In the Crystal Palace, Colonel Conley was showing around a tour group of a few men, their wives, and a few teen-agers, all dressed nicely. As McKittrick passed them, Conley was saying: '... This operation is on constant alert here twenty-four hours a day so your constituency and your homes are always safe. For example, last week we had the governor of New Jersey up here with his people. He wanted to know why we were at DEFCON 4, as we are now ...'

McKittrick turned to Pat. 'Why *are* we at DEFCON 4?'

Pat answered in a businesslike manner, but her eyes betrayed a spark of fear. 'The Soviets saw our bombers scramble with their *own* satellites. They went on alert themselves. We've told them it was an exercise, but we're waiting for them to relax their posture before we do.'

McKittrick shook his head wearily. 'Tour groups. I'd outlaw them in this place. Especially right now.'

'You know, John, you're a real pain when things don't go your way,' Pat said.

'People think my machines came within an inch of starting World War III and you wonder why I'm in a black mood!'

'Nobody thinks it was your machines, John. They know it was that kid.'

'But it was my machines that let him in, and it's my neck in the noose, so, Miss Healy, if I have your permission, I'd like to remain in my black mood for the time being.'

'It would just be a lot more pleasant if you would relax a little.'

'You're taking advantage of our relationship, Pat. Remember, I'm still your boss.'

Pat did not comment on that. She strode along with him quietly.

'Well, don't clam up, Pat. Everytime we have a minor locking of horns, you act like an *iceberg*.'

'Drop dead, Mr McKittrick.'

Oh, God, McKittrick thought. Another cold war. It was almost as though they were married or something. McKittrick didn't like the idea of domestic-type problems at work, which put him in an even fouler mood.

Boy, would he like to get his hands on that kid. It was all that little bugger's fault!

They walked in silence through the briefing room door. Paul Richter, looking even more burned out than usual, stood by a blackboard filled with program specifications and circuitry schematics, chalk dust all over his sweater.

The room smelled of coffee and cigarette butts.

Seated at the table were the head honchos, dressed up in their best professional frowns. Berringer was staring daggers at everybody. Dougherty, Cabot, and Watson waited patiently for Richter to finish his lecture, their glazed expressions indicating their lack of comprehension. A man McKittrick did not know sat beside them in rumpled civilian clothes with eyes that looked like they'd been open for a long time.

Richter sat down and sighed dramatically. '... Mr Cabot,

you've got to believe us, it was a *one-in-a-million* shot – there was an open line at our space division in Sunnyvale. The phone company messed up.'

Richter glanced at McKittrick. Relief flooded his face.

Cabot said, 'John, good to see you. This is George Wigan. George is with the FBI. As you might have heard, they've brought the boy here for questioning.'

McKittrick extended his hand; Wigan took it, reluctantly and coldly.

'How did it happen, Paul?'

Richter said, 'Well, he penetrated the war-game subsystem using a password left in by the original programmer. No one knew the password was in there.'

Wigan shook his head. 'The kid claims he was looking for a toy company!'

General Berringer snorted. 'Likely story!'

McKittrick leaned against the table, assuming his very best professional veneer, combined with a dash of weary authority. 'Paul, I want you to find that password and remove it. Put a tiger team on it – and beef up security around the WOPR.'

'A little goddamned late for *that*, don't you think?' Berringer said belligerently.

Cabot glanced at McKittrick. 'Yes, John. There *is* some real concern about a breakdown in security here.'

McKittrick tried to keep his nervousness out of his voice. 'Well, gentlemen, I think we're being a bit naive here ... I mean, you don't *really* think some high school punk could just pick up the phone and do this on his own, do you?' He banged the table with his fist and met Cabot's eyes dead on. 'The kid's working for somebody. He's *gotta* be!'

Wigan coughed, and wiped his nose with a handkerchief. He flipped through some notes. 'Well, he *does* fit the profile perfectly. Intelligent but an underachiever ... alienated from his parents ... few friends ... We got a lot of help of this from the vice-principal from the boy's school. Guy by the name of Kessler. Fine fellow. We all agree that this David Lightman character is a classic case for recruitment by the Soviets.'

McKittrick said, 'I'll be able to determine that, I think. Just let me have a talk with the boy.'

Cabot smiled. 'Terrific. But we need some answers, fast, John. The President wants blood – and if it's commie blood – well, let's just say that we'll *all* come out looking a lot cleaner.'

'But what if he's not associated with any Soviet intelligence efforts?' Watson said, looking over at Wigan. 'Any insight yet on why anyone – especially a bright boy like this – would jeopardize the lives of millions?'

'No, sir.' Wigan's cynical gaze swept the room. 'The little jerk says he does this sort of thing for *fun*.'

John McKittrick thought, *I'd like to show the kid some fun!*

Ve haff vays of making you talk, Herr Lightman! the voice said ominously in David's head as he nervously glanced around the infirmary room, waiting for something to happen. As soon as they'd brought him to this subterranean place, they'd locked him up here in the sickroom. Probably because it was the only room in the NORAD facility that had a lock. Still, as David looked at the white cabinets around him, uncomfortable images of scalpels and syringes filled his head.

As though he hadn't been scared enough already. The handcuffs biting into his wrists ... The hulking ex-football linebackers the United States used for agents, looking as though they'd as soon chew him up with their Pepsodent molars as take him to their bosses ... The jet plane ... The helicopter ... And worse, the terrible images that his imagination was conjuring up!

Good day, Mr and Mrs Lightman! I'm from the F B I. We have your son in custody, and he's due to fry in the chair tomorrow morning for treason.

Good riddance, his father would say.

Oh wonderful, his mother would cry, *I can sell my story to the* National Enquirer!

Well, he was in the right place, anyway. David Lightman felt like throwing up.

And he had thought 'Kaiser' Kessler was bad.

David sat on the examination table. The sanitary paper covering it had torn from David's scrunching around. He felt like crying, but he was too scared to do anything but stare at his handcuffs.

Beep, beep, beep ...

David started. The sounds came from the door. The unlocking codes. David Lightman waited, his heart in his mouth, thinking about that story they had just read in his English class, 'The Lady or the Tiger?' Which would walk through that door now?

A burly Air Police sergeant pushed the door open. 'Here you go, sir. We're keeping him in here just in case ... I dunno, he seems harmless enough to me.'

'Thank you, Sergeant,' said another, older man. A corduroy jacket with elbow patches and a knit tie gave him a friendly, casual look. A well-clipped mustache, as brown as his eyes, rode neatly between smile lines. *Well,* thought

David, *at least he doesn't have a whip or a cattle prod*.

The new arrival looked at David appraisingly for a moment, unable to conceal his surprise, as though thinking to himself, *This skinny little shrimp was the guy who almost started World War III?*

'Hello, David,' the man said. 'I'm John McKittrick. I run the computer facility here.'

David opened his mouth to speak, but realized his mouth was too dry and his voice would probably come out sounding like a frog's croak. He let a nod suffice.

'Sergeant, would you come in please and get these cuffs off him?'

'Sure, Mr McKittrick,' the man said, jangling some keys as he strode forward and expertly released David's hands of their restraint.

'David,' McKittrick continued in a smooth voice, 'I called your parents. I told them you're fine and that we haven't filed any charges yet in this unfortunate business.' The man frowned thoughtfully. 'But I also said we'll need a little time to sort this whole thing out.'

'How much time?' David managed to rasp.

'That, David, depends on how well you cooperate.'

The handcuffs were gone. David rubbed the circulation back through his wrists. Pins and needles!

McKittrick addressed the guard. 'Tell the O.D. I'm taking him for a little walk.' He turned to David and smiled. 'Come on, David, we'll be more comfortable in my office.'

David hesitated, wondering if he wasn't safer here.

'C'mon, fellow! We'll have a good chat. Lotta interesting stuff out there I can show you. You'll like my office much better, I promise you.'

'How thoughtful,' David said, surprised at his potential for sarcasm even in this situation.

'Aren't I, though?' McKittrick smiled and put a fatherly arm around David as he guided the boy toward the computer facilities.

Wait a minute, David thought. *McKittrick. John McKittrick!*

'You used to work with Stephen Falken, didn't you?' David couldn't help but let the awe creep into his voice.

'I started out as Falken's assistant. Who told you that?'

'I read the article you wrote together on poker and nuclear war.'

'The one on bluffing?' McKittrick seemed genuinely impressed. 'Yeah, that upset a few people.'

'He must have been an *amazing* guy.'

McKittrick seemed to be a bit bothered by that thought. 'I made a few contributions to his work . . . *quite* a few. Stephen Falken was brilliant, certainly, but he was a flake. He never really understood that his work could have practical uses, that it didn't have to exist in some ethereal never-never land, that it could be used in the real world. I'm the one who made the changes and adaptations, David. I'm the hardware man.' He opened a door for the boy. 'Ah, here we are David. The computer center. We've been remodeling. State-of-the-art stuff here.'

David caught his breath. Beautiful, so beautiful . . . streamlined metal and glass, pulsing with power and knowledge . . . what genius danced within these machines stretching to a vanishing point in the distance? What magical secrets? Pools of blue and green light defined occasional work areas where teams of white-coated technicians huddled like sorcerer's apprentices. As they walked through the corridor of machinery, a frisson moved up David Lightman's spine.

They strode past a row of squat red cylinders sitting on foam cushions.

'Oh, wow!' David said. 'That's a Cray 2!'

'Ten of them,' McKittrick said.

'I didn't know they were out yet.'

McKittrick almost preened. 'Only ten. Come on, I want to show you something.'

McKittrick stopped by an old-looking machine attached to arrays of more modern peripherals by glowing strands of optical fibers. Across the faded green housing were the letters *WOPR*. Three smoked-glass panels partitioned it from the rest of the center.

'This is the machine that runs Falken's game program.'

David blinked. 'Joshua's in there,' he murmured. He looked up at McKittrick. 'You still use the original hardware?'

McKittrick nodded and leaned against the housing. 'Falken created a new programming language for the game player. He designed this machine for the program. It still works, beautifully. We've increased its power and memory by a factor of ten thousand.'

'And let me get this right ... this just plays the games ... How does it influence what goes on in the rest of this place?'

'The generals I work with,' McKittrick said, 'base every decision they make on what comes out of this machine. But they don't understand it. They're a little afraid.'

'But what goes into the machine?' David wanted to know.

'Come on, I'll show you.'

McKittrick led him past an open circular area where several workers in white jumpsuits sat at a console before

116

large screens. As they began walking up a metal stairway to a mezzanine level overlooking the cavernous Crystal Palace, David watched the screens with absolute fascination. A sequence of computer-enhanced images flashed on the screen, each showing greater detail ... gradually revealing the outlines of a city ... even buildings ... until a busy urban intersection could be made out. An overturned donkey cart caused a traffic jam.

McKittrick paused and looked at the images. 'Beirut, I think, David.'

'Incredible.'

'You've heard the Pentagon joke that our satellites can read the license plate of a Volga from a hundred miles up, or tell which Russian soldiers shaved each morning? Well, it's not far from the truth.'

'The *technology* ...'

'KH-11 digital imaging satellites. The Big Bird satellite. The Close Look satellite. And the Chalet ... among others. They're all watching the world, David, and all the information transmitted from them goes through our computers, including Falken's WOPR, and then onto our screens. Falken's game program is a vital focus ... and your intrusion shifted that focus, apparently, so that games it kept to itself were thrust up on the screen, confusing us.'

'God.'

McKittrick shrugged. 'Well, we'll just have to make sure this kind of thing doesn't happen again. You did quite effectively point out a weakness none of us was aware of.' McKittrick looked around him. 'The whole world may become dependent on computers ... but it will certainly therefore be dependent on the people who *know* computers.' He looked at

117

David. 'I think you've felt it, David . . . alone in your room . . . crashing systems, breaking codes, accessing other worlds . . . you've felt the power, haven't you, David?'

'Yes,' David said. 'I guess that's a part of why I did it.'

'Imagine how we feel here.' McKittrick continued on up to the mezzanine. 'Now, David,' he said, pointing to a sign. 'See that sign there? That's our current defense condition. It *should* read DEFCON 5 . . . that indicates peace. But because of your little stunt, we're still on DEFCON 4. If we hadn't caught onto the fact that what we were seeing was not an attack but a simulation, we might have gone to DEFCON 1, and that would have meant a world war.'

David had no comment. He felt empty inside . . . it was too much to take in all at once.

'Now, you broke in,' McKittrick continued, 'because you wanted to play a game, right?'

'That's right,' David said.

'My office is right up here.'

David followed the man into a well-appointed office with a view of the Crystal Palace. A monitor glowed in the darkness of indirect lighting.

'Have a seat.'

David sat, as McKittrick went to an icebox.

'Coke? Root beer? Mountain Dew?'

'Coke.'

McKittrick popped the top of the can and handed the drink to David. David gulped. He hadn't realized how thirsty he was.

'Why, David, after you saw what had happened on the news . . . why did you break in again?'

David choked. Fizz spumed up his nostrils.

118

McKittrick kept on. 'You *knew* how serious it was, didn't you?'

'I *didn't* do it again,' David insisted. 'I even threw the phone number away!'

'I know. We found it in the trash.'

'Joshua called *me* back.'

'David, you can pull that on some dumb FBI man . . . don't try it on me.'

'But it's true – it still thinks we're playing a game.'

'A game.' McKittrick sat down and perused some notes. 'David, who were you supposed to meet in Paris?'

'Paris?' Then he remembered. Jennifer had wanted that romantic trip. He'd booked it and had forgotten to cancel. 'Oh, no . . . you don't understand . . .'

'You made reservations for two. Who else knows about this, David?' McKittrick said in a soft voice.

'Nobody,' David replied. *I don't want to get Jennifer into this*, he thought.

McKittrick suddenly cut his act and eyed him coldly. 'Why don't I believe you?' The look sent chills through David.

He put the Coke on the desk and said, 'Maybe I shouldn't say anything until I talk to a lawyer.'

McKittrick stood up and bent over the desk. 'Forget that lawyer crap. You're not going anywhere until I get the truth out of you. A snot-nosed kid just doesn't do this to my machines, you understand? It can't be just you. You've got to be working with somebody!'

'How many times do I have to tell you!' David said despairingly. 'I did it as a challenge. I just got *lucky* . . . !'

'David, this isn't high school. Your actions have consequence ... far greater than you might imagine. Now I'm trying to help you —'

'Look, I told them ten times, I broke into the system to play a game. It's not *my* fault your guys can't tell the difference between a simulation and a Russian missile attack.'

The phone rang. McKittrick picked it up. 'Yeah?'

A look of alarm invaded his eyes. *'What?'* he said disbelievingly. 'Right. I'll be down.' He put the phone down. 'You don't move. Understand? You stay *right there.'*

'Where could I go?' David said. 'I just want to get this straight with you guys.'

McKittrick wasn't listening. He hustled out of the room. David went to the window. He watched as McKittrick almost ran to the command balcony, where a bunch of military bigwigs were conferring. A heated discussion commenced that had enough body English to win a bowling tournament.

David watched the people who ran the systems that could destroy the world, and he shook his head in disbelief.

Below him, McKittrick took a deep breath. His forehead was damp, and he felt as if little fires had been lit here and there in his body.

He barely noticed Cabot approaching the command balcony.

'What's going on?' Cabot demanded in a style that was used to getting immediate answers.

Paul Richter looked like McKittrick felt. His tie was off now, and there were sweat stains under his arms. 'There's just been a very serious penetration into our WOPR execution order file.'

'Huh?' Cabot said. 'Tell me that again. This time in *English*!'

Even the normally stone-faced Berringer was clearly rattled. 'I'll give it to you in English. Somebody's gotten into this boy's system and stolen the codes that can launch our missiles. Simple enough.' Berringer was clearly past all need to be polite to government figures. He looked as if he were about to have a fit of apoplexy.

Time to cool things down here, McKittrick thought. 'I'd like to point out there's no immediate danger. The system won't accept the launch codes unless we're at DEFCON 1.'

Cabot, however, would not be appeased. 'Who *did* this?'

McKittrick fielded that question before anyone else had the chance. 'We don't know yet. That kid must be working with someone on the outside. But I can *change* those codes in less than an hour.'

'I don't know what they're trying to pull here,' Berringer said, 'but I don't want our bombers on the ground when it happens.' He turned to Colonel Conley, stationed at the communications line. 'Get SAC. Let's go to DEFCON 3.' He turned to Cabot. 'The blasted Soviets are up to *something*. Using a *kid*! Unbelievable.' He turned to an aide. 'Get me immediate updates on Soviet submarine deployment. I want to see what those characters are up to!'

No good, as usual, thought McKittrick. *So much for the START agreement.*

Orders were executed. The scoreboard switched from DEFCON 4 to DEFCON 3.

David Lightman looked down at the military and civilian folk on the command balcony, clearly not in great moods.

Obviously something was up. Something big, something serious.

The Russians had nothing to do with this and David Lightman knew it. But those idiots didn't believe him. They were acting crazy.

He had to prove it to them.

As soon as McKittrick had led him through the office door, David Lightman had noticed the computer terminal. Like a dog to a bone ... David could almost sense its presence even now.

It gave him an idea.

Quickly he sat down at the terminal. Nice. Modern. Now, where was the 'on' switch. Ah!

The screen came to life. Immediately after, a command surfaced, like a message floating up from a fortune-telling eight ball.

LOG ON.

David typed in: JOSHUA 5.

He prayed they hadn't changed the code word. He hadn't told them what it was, but they did not know that he had gained access through a back door and –

The letters appeared quickly: GREETINGS, PRO-FESSOR FALKEN.

HELLO, David typed desperately. ARE YOU STILL PLAYING THE GAME?

OF COURSE, Joshua answered. I SHOULD REACH DEFCON 1 AND LAUNCH MY MISSILE IN 28 HOURS. WOULD YOU LIKE TO SEE SOME PRO-JECTED KILL RATIOS?

A series of numbers flashed, but David hit the override button.

The screen cleared.

IS THIS A GAME OR IS IT REAL? he said.

WHAT'S THE DIFFERENCE? replied the Joshua5 program.

David was stunned. Of course! The computer program had no concept at all of reality. It didn't know that if it continued, civilization would end, millions of people would die. It only knew that it was supposed to play a game, and to play that game, it had to launch those missiles!

GAME TIME ELAPSED: 45 HRS. 32 MINS. 25 SECS.

ESTIMATED TIME REMAINING: 27 HRS. 59 MINS. 39 SECS.

YOU ARE A HARD MAN TO REACH. COULD NOT FIND YOU IN SEATTLE AND NO TERMINAL IS IN OPERATION AT YOUR CLASSIFIED ADDRESS. ARE YOU ALIVE OR DEAD TODAY?

Hey! What was this?

STOP PLAYING, David typed. I'M DEAD.

IMPROBABLE, the computer responded. THERE ARE NO DEATH RECORDS ON FILE FOR FALKEN, STEPHEN W., AND NO TERMINAL IS IN OPERATION AT YOUR CLASSIFIED ADDRESS.

This could really be something, thought David. *If I could get a hold of the man who . . .*

WHAT CLASSIFIED ADDRESS? David typed in.

The monitor responded immediately.

DOD PENSION FILES INDICATE CURRENT MAILING AS:
DR ROBERT HUME
5 TALL CEDAR ROAD

'He's really alive,' David said, excited. 'Stephen Falken is alive!' He bent back over the computer to see if he could pick out anymore information, but was interrupted by the opening of the door.

'Hey, watch out! Get him *away* from that thing!' a voice squawked. David flicked the machine off, before anyone could see what he was up to. He turned and saw that the federal agents who had 'escorted' him there, Wigan and Stockman, were moving through the door like a couple of runners sprinting from a starting line. They grimaced angrily as they grabbed David and hauled him away from the monitor.

'You'd think they'd *know* better than to leave him in here alone,' Stockman said, his hold around David's bicep quite a bit stronger than necessary.

'Just checking out the the equipment, guys!' David said. 'No harm done. Look, can't I please talk to Mr McKittrick?'

Wigan pulled out a set of cuffs. 'I told 'em to keep the bracelets on!'

David gestured down to the command balcony. 'He's right down there. It's an emergency! It'll just take a minute, please!'

Wigan's face was death on ice. 'David Lightman,' he said, 'I'll be escorting you to federal authorities in Denver, where you'll be placed under arrest pending indictment for espionage.' His thin lips seemed frozen in a scowl of contempt.

David's heart leapt. 'Espionage? No! There's something weird going on here, and it's got nothing to *do* with espionage! I can explain it to Mr McKittrick if you just –'

Wigan pulled a piece of paper from his jacket and thrust it into David's face. 'Lightman, this is a Miranda. It informs you of your rights. Read it over. Then if you'll just sign it for me.' He smiled maliciously as he picked up a pen from the desk. 'Please.'

'I'm telling you –'

'The man asked "please" real nice,' said Stockman, increasing the strength of his grip. 'Now, are you going to make me ask "please" not so nicely?'

David groaned. 'Okay, okay!' He accepted the paper and looked at it. *You have the right to remain silent. You have the right . . .* God, it was just like on *Hill Street Blues*!

'I'm telling you guys,' he said as he signed, 'the system is messed up. The WOPR is playing a game . . . it's trying to start a nuclear war as a *game*!'

'Come on, Stockman. We'll stick him where we had him before, and this time he's off limits to that McKittrick fellow.'

'I just had a thought, Wigan. You think maybe the Russkies got through to him via his computer? We better put a check on this . . . Half the hackers in America may be potential Soviet agents!'

'I'll tell you one thing,' said Wigan. 'I'm gonna take that Atari away from *my* kid!'

Chapter Eight

David Lightman tried to sit still. He tried to use his fear to keep him in place on the chair in the infirmary behind the locked door. After all, there was nothing more he could do; chances were, if he made one more squeak, those FBI agents would order that MP airman to draw his .38 and put a few permanent bugs in Mr and Mrs Lightman's troublesome program.

He tried to breathe steadily, to put a hold on his frustration. After all, the men here at NORAD, in the Crystal Palace, were the experts. Surely they knew what they were doing. Maybe they even realized that, if necessary, and if Stephen Falken were indeed still alive and at that Oregon address, they could always call in the Prime Programmer.

But then, what if they *didn't* . . .

David sprang up from the chair and began pacing furiously, frustration tying him up in knots.

What if they *didn't* call Falken? What if they had too much pride to check into the matter, to realize that somehow Falken's brilliant machine, programmed to learn, had almost come alive and was determined to play out the insane game that David had begun? The thing was, these authority goons were just like most of the rest: his father, 'Kaiser' Kessler, Mr Ligget, his pastor – incomplete beings who thought they had control of their little sections of reality; stubborn, prideful men who thought they had the rules in their pockets.

Maybe even if he did get to speak to the man, Dr McKittrick wouldn't believe him. He had that element to him, the way he had spoken about Dr Falken, the disrespect. The world was just a bunch of hungry egos, it seemed, scrabbling and biting for power.

Let them go right ahead, thought David Lightman. We're doomed anyway. Even if we get through this mess, who knows what might happen. The President might go off his rocker and fancy himself the town sheriff in a shootout with black-hat Andropov. 'Take that, ya varmint!' And *kazoom*, there go the Titan IIs and the Poseidons and Lances and Minutemen and *kaboom, kaboom, kaboom!* A Russian might dump a bottle of vodka on a control panel and shoot off SS-17s and -18s toward Hackensack, New Jersey.

With these clowns it was inevitable. Eventually there would be a thermonuclear war. And the funny thing about it was that David Lightman was now in the safest place of all – he'd survive.

Of course, he realized he'd have to live with the knowledge that he had been the one who started the ball rolling, the one who had gummed up the machinery, the one who had pushed the first domino. And what kind of world would be left? He'd always figured that if there *were* a nuke war, he'd be one of the first to go, and he didn't think of it much anyway.

Then he thought of Jennifer Mack. Something went funny inside of him. A pang, an ache. She would be gone, then, and

127

a world without her didn't seem like much of a world at all.

Dammit, he thought. *Lightman, you're the one who started all this! Take the rap, the finger of responsibility is on your nose, boy.*

It's your fault. Your never-never-land of computers is attached to a world of flesh and blood and death and you are not Peter Pan!

It was his fault, and he alone knew what was wrong. Also, he alone knew that unless Stephen Falken was brought into this, things really could go wrong. But they thought he was a spy, and they sure as hell weren't going to listen to him . . .

David stopped pacing.

He knew he had to do something . . . or die trying.

Somehow, he had to get in touch with Anderson Island, Oregon.

Somewhow, he had to contact Dr Stephen Falken. Only Falken could convince these people that it was Joshua that was doing this, that it wasn't the Russians, futzing with their computers.

Well, that was decided. Now, how could he get out of here? He surveyed the room for the umpteenth time, but this time with a clear intent: escape. Wait a minute. That metal panel over there – measuring approximately two feet by two feet – that probably controlled the electronic mechanism that locked the door. David examined it closely. It was screwed tightly into the wall. David broke a fingernail testing just how tightly it was fastened. A Phillips screwdriver was needed.

Under the room's sink was a line of drawers. David tried them. Bottom, locked. Second, locked. Third, locked. But the top one slid open and David stared hopefully into it. Nothing but the usual disposable doctor's supplies: a roll of Bounty paper towels, spools of gauze and adhesive tape, tongue depressors (*open wide and say ahh, door!*). Absolutely nothing of use. Just his luck.

He slammed the door shut and sighed.

Hold your horses, he thought. Was that a glint of metal?

Rapidly, David tugged the door open again and tossed away the paper and other stuff. Sure enough, bingo! A batch of disposable syringes was there – no good. Some Ace bandages – no good; a small cassette recorder – no good; a stethoscope – no good; a pair of tweezers . . .

Cassette recorder!

His memory replayed the sounds that had come from the door when the guard had opened it to allow McKittrick entrance. He'd heard about doors like that. In fact, come to think of it, he had read a few articles about them in *Popular Mechanics*.

David took out the recorder. A hand-held Sony job. Expensive. Only the best foreign stuff for our country! He took the earphone and plugged it into his ear. He turned on the 'play' button.

'Patient's pupils are dilated . . . consistent with recent use of marijuana,' a doctor's voice pronounced.

David turned it off, picked up the tweezers, then went to the door. There was a chance this might work! If it did, old Sting would certainly be proud of him.

With the tweezers, and a good deal of sweat, he managed to unscrew the panel. Carefully, so as to not make a sound, he unfastened it and stared into the multicolored spaghetti of wiring.

It took him a good five minutes to connect the recorder and get the panel back in place, but it was good work. The problem was, there was no way to test it.

He went to the door again, and put his ear against it.

Outside, he could hear the guard talking to that pretty nurse at the desk.

'No, thanks, Corporal, tonight I have to do my laundry,' the nurse was saying.

The guard was being insistent. 'Well, I'm off tomorrow night too. Maybe we can go to the smorgasbord. It's all you can eat, Nancy.'

David took a breath, then pounded as hard as he could on the door. Then he took the recorder and placed the built-in microphone next to the metal panel.

He heard the guard's footsteps approaching. 'What do you want?' the man asked.

'There's no toilet in here, and I have to go to the bathroom. It's a long ride to Denver!' David said.

The guard hesitated.

'Look, I gotta go bad. You want me to smell up your nice clean sanitary infirmary?' David said, not having to affect the strain in his voice.

Come on! Open the door or I'm cooked!

The guard took his sweet time to decide, but finally he began to punch out the code on the dial next to the door.

Beep . . . beeep . . . bip . . . beeep . . . bip . . . blip.

The door swung open, and the young corporal stood, eyes wary, his hand on his pistol.

David said quickly, 'Please let me talk to Dr McKittrick. I have to tell him –'

A pained expression crossed the corporal's blandly regular features. 'Look, kid. No one is supposed to talk to you. The FBI guys are gonna be here any minute. Now, do you have to take a leak or don't you?'

'No,' said David.

'Sheesh,' the guard said. 'I'll tell ya kid, I'll be glad when you're gone.'

'So will I,' said David.

The guard shrugged contemptuously and closed the door.

David waited for the guard's footsteps to fade, then pulled the panel back off the wall. It slipped from his sweat-slick hands. He caught it just before it clattered to the floor.

C'mon, klutz, he told himself. *Get with it!*

Cautiously he placed the panel on the floor, then rose up and peered into the control wiring and retrieved the cassette recorder, wired into the mechanism with the earphone cord.

He rewound the tape and moved the jack from 'input' to 'output'. This was it!

His forefinger hit the 'play' button.

Faint tones sounded – an exact repetition of the unlocking sequence. The door lock hummed quietly and clicked. Then, with malicious glee in his eye, he pulled a very important wire.

How about that, Jim Sting! David thought with satisfaction, as he carefully opened the door and peeked out. Down the corridor, the nurse was laughing. The guard had his back to David, leaning over and listening to her heart with a stethoscope.

'Your mouth says, "No ... no ... no," ' the corporal was saying. 'But your heart says, "Yes! Yes! Yes!" '

Time to get *out!*

David slipped through the door into the hallway, quietly closing the door behind him, making sure it locked. This should keep them occupied for a while. Probably they'd think it had stuck!

Desperately he looked around. Where to now? Out of that guard's sight, that was for sure. He raced down the hall, dodging around a corner. He found himself in a foyer complete with elevator doors.

Ping! One of the lights went out. *Oh, geez!*

David ducked into a door under an exit sign.

'I don't know what we're going to do with him,' Wigan was saying as he left the elevator. 'The kid's under-age.'

'If he's been doing what we think he's been doing,' said Stockman, 'maybe we can get a special act of Congress.'

Panic took hold of David Lightman and propelled him down the concrete steps.

Moments blurred into minutes of metal and gray concrete and red exit signs, until David puffed to a halt, realizing that he couldn't go any farther down.

Breathless, he looked around to where his flight had deposited him.

Giant springs connected the ceiling to the floor here – this must be the rockbed upon which the whole complex was perched! Up ahead was a place where the ceiling sloped down to a dark crawl space. It didn't look particularly safe or inviting, but it was the only way to go.

David got down on all fours and began to crawl.

Wigan and Stockman waited with the guard by the locked infirmary door.

'What's up,' asked the technician they had called.

'This lock ... it must be stuck,' said the corporal, pointing to the locking mechanism with its series of numbered buttons. 'Think you can open it?'

'Sure. Just a minute,' the technician said, jauntily chewing a wad of gum. He put his tool kit down, selected a couple of pieces, and set to work while Wigan and Stockman waited impatiently.

It took longer than just a minute, and the FBI agents commented on this quite often and quite vocally.

'You know,' the technician said finally, looking up from the tangled mess of screws and wiring. 'I think it's jammed from inside.'

Wigan blew up. He stepped forward and pounded on the door. 'Come on, Lightman! You're just making it harder on yourself!'

'I got it,' said the technician. 'Here it comes.'

The door swung open. David Lightman was nowhere to be seen.

'Gee, folks,' said Colonel Conley, rejoining the tour group, a nervous, apologetic smile on his face. 'I've just been informed that they're cleaning the floors in the computer center. We don't want anyone to slip and hurt themselves, so we're going to end the tour right here. Now, if I can ask you all to board the bus kind of quickly, we'll have a complimentary beverage waiting for each of you down the hill at the officers' club.'

David Lightman peered out at the forest of legs from his hiding place under one of the machines. The crawl up here had been strenuous, and he was just regaining his breath.

How much longer did he have before they found out he had escaped the infirmary room? Not long, certainly. He'd been on the run for a good five minutes, maybe more. Any moment the storm troopers would come screaming out like a bunch of Jack Kirby cartoon characters, cigars dangling impossibly from apelike teeth, machine guns blazing.

'He's still alive, Sgt Fury!'

'This one's for the Gipper, Commie!'

Ker-blam, ker-blam, ker-blam!

Suddenly, David wished he didn't have such a comic-booky imagination.

The pairs of loafers and high-heeled wedgies started moving on, and David rallied his strength. Blending in somehow with this tour group was his only shot. Too bad he wasn't wearing fancier clothing. He was going to stick out like a sore thumb.

David scrambled out of his hiding place as the last of the tour group – a slim woman in a tight skirt, her face displaying too much lipstick and mascara – turned a corner.

He was about to follow her when a hand hooked on to his shoulder and spun him around.

Oh, geez, this is the end, he thought.

'Hold it right there,' said a man in khakis with a sergeant's stripes and bad breath. 'Caught you, didn't I?'

David couldn't speak.

The sergeant wiped a hand over his thin lips, his hawklike eyes seemingly staring into the depths of David Lightman's soul. 'You kids think you can get away with anything. You know you're not supposed to leave the group. Now get going!'

David couldn't believe his luck. 'Y-yes ... yes, sir, sorry, sir,' he stammered.

The sergeant let him go. He hobbled after the tour group, who were being led to their bus. He fully expected another heavy hand to fall on him at any moment. He sat in the back of the transport, trying to look innocuous as the tour guide gave a hurried farewell to the group and then raced away.

An alarm blared.

A long-faced guy about David's age turned around.

'Hey, what's happening here?'

'Dunno,' said David stiffly.

'Who are you? I didn't see you along on the tour.'

'I'm a Russian spy, and I gotta get out of here, fast, before they catch me,' said David.

The guy laughed. 'Yeah, and I'm John Riggins, and I'm America's new secret weapon against you Russkies, so ya better watch out.'

The transport vehicle jerked, then moved swiftly away.

In the Crystal Palace, Radar Analyst Adler studied his map. *Oh, no,* he thought. *Not again. What the hell was going on in this world?*

'Twenty-two Typhoon-class subs out of the port at Petro-pavlovsk, rounding the bend at Nordkapp, heading for deep ocean,' he reported. 'Bearing zero nine five degrees.'

Captain Newt was behind him, obviously impressed. 'Boy, it looks like Ivan's getting ready to dig someone a new foxhole.'

Adler said, 'Yeah. I'm beginning to feel like Custer's bugler.'

Inside his office, John McKittrick leaned over his desk with Paul Richter, studying a large spread of wiring diagrams. Pat Healy walked through the door, and he glanced up.

'Hey, if it isn't good news, I don't want to hear it,' he said, seeing her grim expression.

'They lost the kid,' she said. 'He got away.'

135

'What?'

Richter paid no notice, his eyes flicking desperately over the charts.

Pat said, 'They've put out an all-state, all-points bulletin and, of course, they'll get him. But for the moment, he's loose.'

McKittrick stared back down at the wiring charts, and thought about the mess the kid and whoever he was working with had made of his programs, his machines.

He glanced out his window to where the army of analysts and technicians worked frantically at their posts.

He spoke through gritted teeth: 'I hope they blow the little jerk away!'

On the rig's radio, a country and western songstress wailed about a cheating lover.

The grizzled old trucker stared straight ahead onto the black snake of macadam winding up the steep grade. David watched him shift repeatedly.

The tractor-trailer had picked him up on the interstate, and most of the hour's ride had been spent in silence. The old guy just seemed to be enjoying having somebody on the seat beside him, David Lightman thought. What a job, sitting behind a wheel all day, watching a painted white line progress along the highway!

The song changed to 'Convoy'. How appropriate!

David had been sitting, thinking about things, aware now that he had irrevocably changed. The world just couldn't look the same anymore, not after this crazy weekend. It was a lot more complicated than he had figured.

Up till now, David Lightman had considered himself a

mistake, an outcast, an outsider, dancing on the perimeter of things, making faces at the funny goings-on inside the loony bin. But now he realized that he was one of the inmates – had always been one of the inmates – and the struggle going on was his struggle as well. He was a part of everything, and in his arrogance and stupidity he had set in motion a sequence of events that could not only end his little parade but snuff out the lives of millions of other people.

Only because he'd wanted to play a stupid war game! Sting had warned him, but he'd felt invulnerable. Why oh why couldn't he have gone through the usual adolescent-rebellion phase of running away, or forging his mother's signature to excuse slips so he could cut those hateful, boring biology classes? It sure was a lot safer than thumbing his nose at society by fooling around with North America's defense computer.

If they made a movie about him, his fame would beat out Mick Jagger and James Dean for sure. Yeah, he could become a teen heartthrob movie star or even a rock star now.

That is, if he and the world *survived*.

The post-holocaust world would have a song dedicated just to David Lightman: 'You Dropped the Bomb on Me', by the Gap Band.

Ha ha ha, thought David Lightman dourly.

'How come you ain't got no bag or nothin'?' the trucker asked him suddenly, after maneuvering his shift and clutch.

David started. 'Oh! Uhm . . . someone swiped it. Uh . . . how many gears does this thing have?'

'Fourteen speeds,' the man said. His eyes squinted suspiciously, deepening the creases in his craggy face. 'You ain't a runaway, are you?'

'What?' David said, shifting uncomfortably in the battered seat.

'Are you runnin' off from your folks? I mean, you look kinda young.'

'Ain't that the everlasting truth!' David said. 'I can't get served anywhere.'

They rode for a few moments in silence. The trucker glanced around, looking back at his trailer full of canned goods, then into his rearview mirror.

'Cops!' he said suddenly.

'What?' David said, startled.

'Couple of cops pulled me over in Illinois. I swear they looked like they was in grammar school!'

David leaned back, relieved.

'How far you wanna go?'

'What's the next reasonably big city?'

'Place called Grand Junction.'

'That will do fine,' David said.

The driver shrugged and slumped back into silence.

On the radio, the DJ had just started playing 'We Might as Well All Get Stoned', by Mac Davis.

'What city, please?' the directory operator asked nasally.

David said, 'Anderson Island, Oregon ... The number for Dr Robert Hume – H-U-M-E – on Tall Cedar Road.'

David took a bite of his Wendy's cheeseburger as he waited.

The trucker had left him in Grand Junction, as requested. David shivered. There was a cold wind blowing outside the booth.

The operator came back on. 'Checking under Dr Robert Hume, H-U-M-E, on Tall Cedar Road. I find no listing.'

'Does that mean he doesn't have a phone?'

'I'm sorry, I am unable to find any listing,' the operator said impatiently.

'Wait, try Falken, Dr Stephen Falken – F-A-L-K-E-N – same address.'

There was a pause.

C'mon! C'mon, David Lightman thought, his square hamburger cooling, oozing mustard and ketchup in his tightening grip.

'I find no listing for a Dr Stephen Falken, F-A-L-K-E-N, on Tall Cedar Road, Anderson Island.'

David Lightman hung up, and began to think desperately.

Dance, dance, dance, I wanna dance all night, the record player demanded. *Let's do the dance of love, bay-bee, until the morning light!*

Jennifer Mack lifted her right leg up and down in time to the music. The exercise was called a 'hydrant' because you got down on all fours and lifted up a leg as if you were a male dog doing a number on the local fire plug.

Throbs of synthesizer funk-pop waved through the living room, giving Jennifer the motivating rhythms to move her limber limbs to. Her face glistened with the sweat she had worked up during a half hour of aerobics exercise, and her tank top was soaked with sweat. She preferred Prince's '1999', but this music would do. One of her friends in the aerobics class was urging New Wave on her, but Jennifer Mack tended to prefer the kind of music everybody else liked.

The taped song segued nicely into a Donna Summer/ Giorgio Moroder dance number. Jennifer hopped up and began prancing about in a free-form dance of her own devising.

No one was home. Why not cut loose? Vaguely she wondered if David Lightman danced. Probably not. Jennifer sighed.

She was really getting into a frenzy, when the phone rang. She let it ring for a few times. Maybe it would go away. What a time for someone to call, when she was really getting high on Donna's rolling, insistent synthesized beat.

'Damn!' she said.

She danced over to the extension in the kitchen and picked up the phone. 'Yeah?' she said, not able to keep the annoyance from her voice.

'Jennifer, it's me, David,' said the voice, with a fuzzy long-distance sound.

'David?'

'David Lightman.'

'I know, I know. You sound funny.'

'I'm in Colorado.'

'I wondered why you weren't in school today, David. You didn't miss much in biology. Old Ligget –'

'Listen, Jennifer, this is very important and it's hard to ask but, well . . . can you loan me some money?'

'Money? Sure. When you get back I'll –'

'No, you don't understand. I need you to buy me an airline ticket from Grand Junction, Colorado, to Salem, Oregon. I know it's a lot to ask, and I can't tell you why.'

Jennifer paused, stunned. 'What are you doing in Colorado? I went by your house and your parents were really weirded out, but they wouldn't tell me why. What's happening?'

'I'll tell you later, Jennifer,' said David's voice over the phone. 'I can't talk right now. Will you do it?'

'David, I'm not rich!'

'I know, and you might have to borrow the money from somebody else. But Jennifer, you're the only one I can trust to help me here.'

'Of course I'll help you in any way I can, David,' she said, surprised at how much she really meant it, astonished at the good feeling that swept through her when she said those words.

'Oh, thank you Jennifer.' David's voice conveyed clearly his gratefulness and his relief. 'Listen, when you buy the ticket, tell them I'll pick it up in Grand Junction, but it'll have to be under a different name.'

'Wait a minute,' Jennifer said, reaching for a pencil and a pad from a nearby table. 'I better write all this down.'

'The next plane out will probably be tomorrow, so if you hurry, you'll be able to get the ticket today.'

'Right. Grand Junction, Colorado, to Salem, Oregon. Tomorrow.' Jennifer repeated the words she had written down.

'And you can do it, Jennifer?'

Jennifer smiled. 'David Lightman, you're going to be real surprised at what I can do.'

The smooth, grim, earnest atmosphere of the Crystal Palace had slowly unraveled into a state of efficient, professional chaos, held together by intense concentration.

A weary General Berringer, tie undone, sleeves rolled up, thought about having another coffee and rejected the idea. He was much too wired already. Only three hours of sleep last night. And now that blasted kid Lightman had skipped out on them, thumbing his nose at the best military system in the world.

He looked up at the big board. The symbols for Soviet subs lay in wait off the coast of North America.

DEFCON 3, said the scoreboard.

'Pardon, sir,' said a communications officer, coming up to Berringer. 'We've just received a telex from the State Department.'

'Read it, huh? I gotta save my eyes.'

'Essentially, sir, it states that the Soviets are denying any increase in their submarine deployment. They want to know what the hell we're doing provoking them.'

'Well, they have to be lying,' the general said, pointing up at the board. 'What are *those*, commie whales? Our systems aren't in simulation now, that's for sure. We know they're down there!'

'Yes, sir,' the communications officer said, returning to his station after a salute.

General Berringer sighed. Maybe he *would* have that cup of coffee.

Meanwhile, on the floor of the Crystal Palace, seated at a row of terminals, Technician First Class Roland Moor studied the picture on his monitor.

The screen snowed over with static. Immediately he reacted, cutting on switches, twisting dials. *This shouldn't be happening*, he thought, alarmed.

He turned to Ed Morgan, sitting next to him.

'Hey Ed, check antenna alignment on 0-84. I just lost the picture,' he said.

Ed was going through similar motions. 'I've just lost mine, too.'

'We better get word to the general.'

He made the call to one of General Berringer's aides, who turned to the commander and said, 'Sir, we're not getting signals from two of our early-warning satellites. It could be a malfunction . . . or they could have been knocked out.'

Maybe I'm gonna need a shot of bourbon in that coffee, thought the general tensely.

In the computer center the WOPR machine dreamed its dreams and fought its microchip wars, its optical wires flashing, its machinery humming, its relays clicking softly, like Death snapping skeletal fingers in time to its number-one fave funeral dirge.

Chapter Nine

The seat-belt light came on.

'We're approaching the Salem airport. Please fasten your seat belts and extinguish all cigarettes.'

The captain spoke. It was a commuter flight and there was no stewardess on board. David Lightman buckled his seat belt.

The small jet tilted down, swerving and jumping without the smoothness or stability that big airliners possessed. The abrupt movements made it feel as though they were dropping like a rock. David tensed.

A hefty middle-aged man stubbed out his Tareyton in a nearly full ashtray and blew his last puff of smoke toward the window. 'Yep, we're in the Willamette Valley, son,' the man – a bulk dog-food salesman – told David. 'Only place you can't see mountains in Oregon. And remember, son. It ain't "Wil-uh-met". It's Willamette, dammit.' The man barked a hearty laugh and then turned to watch the descent.

David tried to smile. He felt terrible. He'd slept, or at least *tried* to sleep, at that Colorado airport last night, sitting upright in the waiting room. Breakfast sat uneasily in his stomach, awash in too many cups of airport coffee.

The small runway rose up to meet the wheels of the commuter jet, and the craft eventually taxied to a halt. A ladder was extended to the concrete, and David made his way woozily out, having to walk the last twenty yards to the tiny terminal building.

Now that he was here, he supposed he'd have to hitchhike the rest of the way to Anderson Island. He hadn't thought to ask Jennifer to wire any money. He supposed he should just be happy that the ticket was waiting for him at the booth. Good old Jennifer. If he got through this on the right side of the jail bars, he was going to have to do more than just take the girl to an arcade.

How much time did he have, he wondered as he made his way through the clear spring Oregon day to the sun-flecked glass doors of the terminal. Only until tomorrow. He prayed that even now, the goofs at NORAD had somehow stopped Joshua. The world still existed in much the same way as before – no nuclear craters in Oregon – so he supposed that the brilliant program had not tricked them into launching any missiles yet.

David shivered at the thought. Unbelievable! Even now the concept was too huge to get his mind around. It was –

As he moved through the doors, David saw the policemen immediately, standing by the airport ticket booth. His legs stopped moving. They didn't see him yet. Which way should he go? What should –

A hand grabbed his arm.

He jumped, almost letting out a yelp.

Wide-eyed, he swiveled around. Standing there, looking fresh and pretty as usual, was Jennifer Mack.

'Hi!' she said. 'Oh, I'm so glad you made it!' She gave him

a warm, sisterly hug. 'We were worried you wouldn't make your connection. Aunt Alma tried calling the airline. She's been cooking all day and I've been stuck with our awful cousins from Klamath Falls. You know, the ones who always wear gym clothes and smell so bad.'

'Yeah, well I'm probably not a real rose right now myself.' He guided her to an exit. 'C'mon, let's blow this Popsicle stand.'

'My car's the other way, David,' Jennifer said.

'We can walk around the building. I want to keep my back to the cops. I'm in real trouble, Jennifer.'

'I *know*, David. They came around last night and questioned me! Said they were from the FBI and the FBI could do stuff like that, drag people out of their aerobics exercise and question them.'

They stepped through the automatic doors.

'You shouldn't have come, Jennifer.'

'What do you mean I shouldn't have come? Is it because of that thing you did with my grade?'

'No – I'll explain it to you. You must have driven down.'

'Yeah, early this morning. I'm so grateful my father's such a good guy. He let me. Of course, I told him I'd be visiting my aunt and uncle and –'

'But you've got a car. That's great. And a map, Jennifer?' David said as he followed her to a blue Volvo station wagon. 'You have a map?'

'Sure. Where are we headed?'

'A place called Anderson Island.'

'Why, David?' She unlocked the door for him.

'I'll tell you on the road,' he said and got in.

Later, as they traveled through the Oregon countryside, David tried to explain to Jennifer what had happened.

146

'I was wrong, huh?' she said. 'They *did* find out that we were fooling with that game program. But it wasn't on purpose, David. I know that! I'll tell them that!'

'Thanks, Jennifer, but it's a little too late for that. They don't know anything about you, and that's the way I want to keep it,' David said as the car cut through the farmland toward Anderson Island on the coast.

'You didn't tell them that it was my idea to nuke Las Vegas?' she said. 'Thank you, David.'

'If I told them, they'd have you, right?'

'But they don't have you.'

'Like I said, I escaped. God, if I *was* a trained Russian spy, they'd been in real trouble,' said David, exasperated.

'You ... a Russian spy! Give me a break.'

'I'm not kidding. That guy McKittrick I told you about. He really thinks I'm a pawn of the commies. He just doesn't want to admit that his machines messed up.'

'So anyway, go on. Why are we going to Anderson Island?' Jennifer asked.

'Well, when I was in McKittrick's office, I got a chance to work his computer ... he'd been called out.'

'And just left you there!'

'Must have been an extreme emergency ... anyway, I talked to Joshua again. You know, it's funny, if I hadn't answered that phone, I'd be okay – the phone call from Joshua calling me back.'

'Why did you answer, David?'

'I thought it was you.'

'You mean a dozen other girls don't have your secret phone number?' she asked, a smile in her eyes.

'No, Jennifer, just you.'

'And Joshua.'

'And Joshua. So Joshua tells me that Falken *isn't* dead! And he gave me an address. The Anderson Island address. Before I called you, I tried to call him, under his new name – Robert Hume. Unlisted. So, you know the rest.'

'But why would the obituary say he was dead?' Jennifer wanted to know.

'I guess it was a cover-up. Yeah, a convenient cover-up. Falken left. When these brilliant scientists leave and know too much, they give them new identities. Anyway, that's what Joshua says.'

Jennifer said, 'Yeah, but the military's got to know what's going on. It *is* in their system.'

'That's just it,' said David. 'They don't know Joshua. Falken knows Joshua. And he's the only one who knows what that program can do. It's trying to win the game *we* asked it to play – trying for real. Do you believe me, Jennifer?'

'Yeah ... it's too crazy not to believe. By why can't you tell Joshua that if it starts a war, millions of people will be killed.'

'It's not programmed to be aware of the niceties.'

'But you say it's programmed to learn.'

'It's just a *machine* – a machine full of war games. And its biggest desire right now is to make those war games real.'

'So you think the only one who can stop it is its daddy – Stephen Falken.'

'Who knows ... maybe they've stopped it now. But the maddening thing is that those turkeys won't listen to me. They don't realize what their own machines can do to them. They're so uptight, they're ready to believe that the Russians are doing this. It's almost like they *want* the Russians to be doing this. It's insane!'

'Self-fulfilling prophecy,' Jennifer said, 'we learned about that in psychology.'

'Exactly,' David returned. 'And you know, Jennifer, it makes you really think about the way this world is run. We both grew up just sort of accepting that a few countries who hated each other had the power to wipe out everything. I don't really think we understand what it means. I tell you, *I've* been thinking about it lately, though. Plenty.'

'Yeah, but we've got to protect ourselves. Russia wants to take over the *world*.'

'That's what they teach us,' David said. 'Of course, poor Russia is also dealing with the only country crazy enough to use a nuclear bomb on people – twice. Hiroshima and Nagasaki.'

'I never thought of that.'

'So you've got the two major world powers, scared silly of each other, each with the capability of destroying each other – and much of the rest of the world – a dozen times over. Now other countries have nuclear capability – it's a real tinderbox. And I just lit a fuse.'

'You didn't *know* David. You shouldn't blame yourself.'

'Shouldn't I? Where does the responsibility stop?'

'The fuse was just lying there, waiting for someone. Better you than a real Russian spy!'

'That doesn't take any of the responsibility off *my* shoulders, Jennifer. I was the one who started all this in motion, and I'm the one who's going to have to help to end it. I was just a little jerk who stuck his hands where they weren't supposed to go.'

'I don't think you're a little jerk, David. I like you.'

David smiled softly. 'Thanks, Jennifer. You don't know how much that really helps.'

It was late afternoon when they finally got there.

Anderson Island was the largest of a group of tree-covered islands just off the Oregon coast; large enough to be serviced by a ferry.

Jennifer opted to park by the dock, because she didn't have all that much money and it was cheaper to cross the channel without your car. That was fine by David. He just wanted to get over there any way he could.

They almost missed the last ferry; it was only Jennifer's pleas that convinced the ferryboat captain to wait for them.

That was another one he owed her, David Lightman thought. He would definitely have to take the girl out to dinner.

They stood by the railing. Gulls swooped and hovered. The air smelled strongly of the sea. The sun was just dipping toward the horizon.

'You know,' said David, after a time of silence, 'it's not just a game.'

'Huh?' asked Jennifer. 'What did you say?'

David shook his head. 'Nothing.'

When the ferry docked, David and Jennifer sprinted ahead of the cars and other people onto the island.

Jennifer's feminine charm had coaxed directions from the surly ferryboat captain. 'Just up Woodland Road, 'bout half a mile,' he said, scratching his tangled beard. 'Tall Cedar Road is just a narrow dirt lane.'

They hiked up through the woods, bordered by thick forest that only occasionally yielded glimpses of water. The air smelled good and crisp and clean. It was a beautiful place.

David wished he and Jennifer were there for reasons other than to locate the missing Stephen Falken.

What if they were on the wrong trail. What if Falken *was* dead, and the machine had faulty information in its memory banks. Well, at least he'd have a little more time with Jennifer here on this lovely island.

'There it is,' said Jennifer, pointing to a slanted old sign. 'Tall Cedar Road.'

'Come on. We head back toward the water now, I think.' Encouraged, David increased his pace.

After another half-mile walk they came to a high, over-grown cyclone fence that surrounded a large section of waterfront property. By the entrance stood a battered mail-box, displaying the name 'Dr Hume'.

David was elated. 'This is the place!' he said.

'Terrific. How do we get in, though?' Jennifer wanted to know. She pointed to the heavy chain lock on the fence. 'No tape recorder lock-pick around here.'

David tried the lock anyway. Secure. No sign of any kind of buzzer, either.

'Hullo!' he called out.

No answer.

'Come on, Jennifer. Maybe we can get through by going around on the waterfront side.'

'I dunno, it looks awfully gloomy through there.'

'Just call me Mr Gloom and Doom.'

She didn't laugh, but followed him.

'Good thing I wore jeans,' she said when she caught herself in a patch of briars. 'Too bad they're my good Calvin Kleins.'

'Brooke Shields will never forgive you,' said David, picking off the stickers. 'I'll put in a good word for you, though.'

'You're just too kind,' she said, continuing their noisy progress. 'David, you don't really think she's beautiful, do you?'

'Huh?'

'Brooke Shields.'

'Heck, no. Anyway, she probably can't even break ten thousand on Pac-Man.'

'I can.'

'That's what drives me absolutely crazy about you, Jennifer.'

Jennifer laughed.

They moved on in silence along a dry gully that afforded them easy movement down the slope. Certainly better than scraping past pine needles, thought David. Honeysuckle vine lent a trace of sweetness to the air. A robin stirred among oak leaves, then flapped away, a burst of brown and red. Their footsteps scuffed up gravel, which rattled down the steeper parts of the water-dug gully before them.

Jennifer lost her balance once, but managed to grab hold of twisted oak roots exposed by the erosion.

'Oh, look, David!' Jennifer said. 'Strawberries!'

'Yeah, I'm hungry too,' David muttered. 'We should have thought to bring something along. Too bad we had to race to catch that ferry. We could have brought something.'

'Maybe Mr Falken will give us something to eat.'

'Yeah, if we can *find* him!'

It wasn't long before they could hear the crash of the breakers ahead of them. The scent of the sea was full on the air, and the forest began to thin. David helped Jennifer out of the gully, and they followed the rusty fence the rest of the way down. At the point at which the metal post and mesh met a jumble of rocks, it began a tangled disintegration. The forest stopped there. Between low tide and the forest's verge stretched an outcropping of rocks bordering tidal mud flats. The last of the dusky sun threw reflections from the little pools of water in the mud, like little mirrors sewn into the expanse of brown.

David pointed. 'This is where the property begins. We'll have to move up here this way.' He stepped down. Mud welled up over his foot as he stepped off the rock.

'Yuck!' said Jennifer.

'It's not deep. I'll buy you a new pair of shoes,' David said, offering a hand to help her down.

'No problem,' Jennifer said, gamely squishing into the mud. 'Just a comment. I repeat. *Yuck!*'

The mud sucked on their shoes as they made their way toward dry land. The smell of salt and seaweed was dense here. David's tennis shoes were soaked. Sea chill surrounded his feet and calves.

Jennifer strode on bravely ahead of him, concentrating on her footing. There was certainly a lot more to her than the shallow, pretty teen-ager David had at first perceived her to be – an unfamiliar feeling stirred deep within him as he watched the breeze blow and tangle her hair.

Suddenly a form swooped out of the darkening sky, passing a few feet above Jennifer's head. A seagull? thought David. No. Much too big.

Jennifer flinched back and lost her footing, tumbling into the mud.

'Jennifer!' David cried. He looked up in shocked disbelief as the figure of the creature moved against the light.

Good grief, thought David. *It can't be!*

Leathery wings spanning a good eight feet flapped above, carrying a reptilian body and sharp, scissor-like head higher into the air. It looked like a pterosaur. But it couldn't be, thought David, because pterosaurs had been extinct for more than sixty million years.

Pterosaurs were *dinosaurs*, for God's sake! What was this, the Lost World?

Jennifer was floundering in the muck. David went to help her up. She was a real mess, all of one side pasted with mud. 'Come on,' David said, surprised at his calm. 'We better make for cover.'

Jennifer wordlessly obeyed. Holding on to her arm, they began the difficult business of slopping their way to dry land.

The creature lowered one bony wing, banked, and then glided back. Swiftly it swooped and turned toward them again. 'Get down, Jennifer,' David yelled, pushing her into the mud as he flailed an arm at the pterosaur. He missed and flopped across Jennifer, pushing her face into the mud.

The flying reptile gained height and circled upward along the side of an outcropping of rocks.

'It's going away,' David said, helping Jennifer up.

'What is it?' Jennifer asked, her eyes showing white in contrast to the mud covering her face. She made her way unsteadily to her feet.

David's eyes were fixed on the creature. 'Ptera-something. Pterodactyl, pteranodon. Pterosaur, anyway,' he muttered, relieved that the thing apparently had lost interest in them. 'Whatever it is, it's im –'

His eyes traveled to the top of the rocks where a lone figure stood: a man, *holding some kind of box*. The figure of the flying reptile glided towards the man, who grabbed it out of the air by its talons. The wings folded; the creature was still.

Reality registered in David's mind. 'It's only a *model*!'

'Huh?' said Jennifer, looking up as the man began to descend.

'That man up there is operating it! C'mon, Jennifer. Let's have a talk with this guy.'

Holding muddy hands, they slogged towards the shoreline. As they reached it, a man dressed in dark, rainslick material, holding the folded-up pterosaur and its control box, bounced down from a rock.

'Greetings!' the man said, cocking a thin, delicate face to eye them with cool consideration. 'So sorry that Terry and I put a startle into you. Bit of fun, what?' His English accent seemed dulled by years of Yankee living, but his mannerisms gave him an eccentricity, a flamboyance, a disregard for the conventional that was immediately evident. This guy is straight out of *The Avengers* TV series, David Lightman thought. The man tapped the plastic head of his model. 'Just imagine, once upon a time the sky was filled with these little buggers.'

'Dr Hume, I presume?' Jennifer said snidely, wiping off some of the mud already crusting on her face.

'Ah, you've read my mailbox. Splendid.' He petted his creation fondly. 'Did you know that aeronautical engineers claim that pterosaurs couldn't have flown? Anyway, as you can see, they can fly and fly quite well, although I haven't solved the problems of taking off and landing. But then, they probably dropped from high cliffs where they hung like bats.' He smiled at them hopefully. 'Are either of you paleontologists? I prayed God would send me a paleontologist.'

155

'Sorry,' said David.

'Are you deliberately trespassing?' the man said, clearly disappointed. 'I mean really . . . you are on my property and I didn't invite you.'

'You're Stephen Falken aren't you?' Jennifer said, excited. David had assumed as much, and was quite shocked when the man lost his smile, spun around, and began walking away.

'Just there you'll find a path that leads to a length of chain link fence,' he said, pointing brusquely and impolitely. 'Follow the fence until you come to a gate. Open the gate, exit the property, and please give it a good slam so it locks behind you. Then, if you hurry, you'll just make the six-thirty ferry to the mainland.' His tone was curt, perhaps even nasty.

'Dr Falken,' said David, moving after him. 'I really need your help!'

'Stephen Falken can't help you, old fellow. Stephen Falken, like Marley, is dead as a door knocker and doesn't plan any chain-clanking or imminent Christmas visitations.'

'Doctor . . .' called David. 'I'm here because of Joshua.'

That stopped the man cold. His head jerked up, and he spun around to regard the two teen-agers with a look that had an entirely new expression: astonishment.

'I say, you mean the one who fought the battle of Jericho?'

'No, sir,' said David walking up to him. 'And not your son either, who died. I'm talking about your computer program.'

'Ah,' the man said thoughtfully. 'My goodness, you two are a pair of messes, aren't you. I just happen to have a couple of showers, fluffy towels, and some clean clothes that should fit quite well. A spot of dinner, too, hmmm? Yes, quite.' He spun around, beckoning the two to follow him. 'And then,

156

dears, you perhaps would care to tell me just how two kids know about a top-secret computer program.'

Jennifer smiled. David sighed with relief as they began to follow Dr Stephen Falken home.

Radar Analyst Adler popped a pair of Alka-Seltzers into a glass of water at a safe station to the side of the consoles. His stomach grumbled in anticipation.

Just as his lips were about to touch the fizzing liquid, a warning signal ripped through the air.

His insides seemed to do a double flip as he put the glass back down and ran to his radar scope.

'Take a look at those babies, Adler,' said Jones, one of his assistants.

On the radar scope two blips slowly moved across Alaska, heading toward the continental United States.

'Check for malfunctions,' Adler ordered.

'Already have,' said Jones. 'High confidence. This is for real. And readings just come up 'UNKNOWN'. These aren't ours, Adler.'

Adler swallowed back his fear and clicked on the intercom to the command balcony. 'Regarding warning signal. Radar reports two unknown – repeat, *unknown* – tracks penetrating Alaskan air defense zone. Flight profile suggests Soviet Backfire bombers.' That was just a guess, popping out of his mouth, but he had to say something.

General Berringer on the command balcony felt a surge of adrenaline course through him. He turned to Colonel Conley. 'I want a visual confirmation of this. Scramble some interceptors to take a look.'

'They're up on the board now, General,' Lieutenant

Dougherty reported. Then he turned to his console and fed in some information. 'Their flight path will put them right over PAVE PAWS.'

Colonel Conley said, 'If they knock *that* out, we won't be able to detect a sub launch!'

'Those damned liars,' General Berringer said, pounding the board in front of him, palm down. 'I *knew* they were down there. Let's go DEFCON 2. And I want to talk to that flight leader myself!'

It was but the work of a moment to switch the scoreboard from DEFCON 3 to DEFCON 2, but it took a while longer to get the F-15 jet interceptors up. Soon, however, two more pairs of blips, these known, headed toward the unknown blips.

Flight Leader Bill Johnson sat in his cockpit, clouds and snow and mountains stretching before him, blue sky and space above him. He tapped the radar controls again, and it still gave him the same reading.

'Crystal Palace,' he said into the face mask. 'This is Delta Foxtrot Two Seven. I have negative radar contact. *Repeat.* Negative Soviet aircraft.'

A loud voice boomed in his ear. He had to turn down the volume. 'Two Seven, this is Brass Hat. They're right in front of you. You're almost on top of them!'

Bill Johnson shook his head and looked again. These guys were going nuts. He shrugged and spoke again into his radio transmitter. 'Brass Hat, we've got absolutely zilch out here, General. Bunch of blue sky.'

Back in the command balcony, General Berringer's face was red. 'Now look here, they're on our screens. They must be invisible or something. They must –'

General Berringer stopped in midsentence as the two un-known blips on the big board suddenly raced westward – and disappeared.

'What the devil is going on?' the general said.

Inside the WOPR, Joshua continued to work on its plan for the perfect world war.

The United States would win this one too.

Joshua, after all, was a program designed only to win.

Now it had its chance.

Finally.

Dr Stephen Falken's house was a split-level, modernistic affair, with lots of glass, and a solar-heating unit that Falken claimed to have designed himself. 'Not installed, mind you, though I am quite capable,' he had told them as they crossed the neatly clipped lawn of the estate. 'I simply want to do my bit for the unemployment dilemma, don't you know. Did you realize, my friends, that the government statistics do not take into account the millions of unemployed *dead* people in this country. Frightful!'

The place was fashion-designer beautiful, housekeeper-clean.

Falken nattered on about this insignificance or that ob-scurity, refusing to speak on the subject of Joshua until both his guests had taken their showers, were fitted with dry clothes, and had sampled Falken's steak and kidney pie.

Finally he said, 'Now, please tell me how you two hap-pened upon Joshua.' He raised an elegant eyebrow. 'I take it that one of you is a computer programmer. Quite intelligent, aren't I?'

Jennifer, wearing an oversize red flannel shirt and smelling quite sweet and feminine, sat close to David. She gestured to him. 'He's the one.'

'Ah. And I take it also, Mr Lightman, that you are one of those private computer enthusiasts of this wonderful free-enterprise country known colloquially as a "cruncher". Namely, you stick your computer's nose where it doesn't belong.'

'They think he's a Russian *spy*!' Jennifer said, looking at David with something like amusement, perhaps even pride.

'I was just looking for Protovision. I got Joshua.'

'Whoa. Now, I realize they say that a number of monkeys working at full speed will eventually produce the complete works of Shakespeare, but I find it rather hard to believe that a youngster could just happen upon the backdoor key of my program.'

'I helped with that,' Jennifer said, half in defense of David, half in accepting part of the blame. 'I mean —'

'Now, please, take a nice brisk gulp of your coffee, if you will, Mr Lightman, and start at the beginning.'

David told the story as quickly and succinctly as he could. As Falken listened, he carefully tamped shag-cut tobacco into a briar pipe. They sat in an activity room, replete with Ping-Pong and pool tables, a hearth where a fire now crackled, many bookshelves, and a television set.

As David spoke, Falken reacted in various ways to different sections of the story, puffing Sherlock Holmes-like on his pipe, or scrunching about in his place on the couch, nodding his head, or simply staring off into space, as though he were thousands of miles away.

'They wouldn't listen to me!' David finished up, his cup of cocoa forgotten and cooling on the marble-topped coffee table before him. 'And then when I realized that you were still alive, they wouldn't let me talk to McKittrick. So you see, Mr Falken, I *had* to talk to you. You're the only one who has the chance of convincing them that *Joshua* is trying to start World War III, that it's not the Russians, and certainly not me!'

'Ah yes, though your beady little eyes apparently perked up when they saw "Thermonuclear War" on that games menu, hmmm?'

Jennifer came to David's defense. 'You haven't really been listening, have you? He – *we* thought it was a game.'

'Well, it is, isn't it? And I *have* been listening.' A light of mirth danced in his eyes. 'I loved it when you nuked Las Vegas, my dear. A fine biblical end for the place.'

David spoke in a tone of astonishment. 'But aren't you going to call them and explain what Joshua's doing?'

'He's doing just what he was made to do, David. He's doing just what some Russian computer is no doubt doing.'

Stephen Falken lifted his thin frame from the sofa and went over to a bookcase, where he absently let a finger drift across the back of a number of volumes. 'Children, behold my collection on that most human of games, war. We've been doing it a very long time, you know. It was pure instinct that caused your delight with the notion of playing Joshua's "Global Thermonuclear War", David Lightman. So you need not bask in guilt. We are all bloodthirsty beasts, deep in the bone. We revel in war games, ah yes, we do.' Falken drummed a mime tattoo, and chuckled. 'But before this century, we could have our little games of death and continue stumbling blindly on toward the light of civilization. Alas, then we stumbled upon nuclear energy, and what was it that we first thought to do with it? Why, make *bombs*, naturally, and create the wonderfully Byzantine technology to deliver those bombs accurately across expanses of thousands of miles, and create a controlling network of intricate machinery to function as the brain of this gargantuan technology. The computer, my dears, was not built as the result of an urgent desire of mankind to see a little yellow ball gobbling up dots in a maze. The computer is, in a very real sense, the child of war – and as Wordsworth says, the child is the father of the man.'

'Huh?' said Jennifer.

'And I am the father to Joshua,' Falken continued. 'You see, I too had my blind obsession, I, a gentleman like Al Einstein himself, who first pointed out that uranium or plutonium could pack a mighty big wallop, merely from an almost deranged fascination with and genius for mathematics. Perhaps it is all some magnificent death wish, buried deep in the collective consciousness of us all.'

'All you have to do,' said David, 'is to give them a *call*.'

Falken put his hands in his pockets, and gave David a desperate smile.

'Listen, children. Once upon a time, a long while ago, there lived a magnificent race of animals who dominated the world through age after age.'

He swiveled and went to a collection of V H S tapes, selected one, and popped it into a Sony atop the R C A console. A collection of classic portrayals of film, video, and cartoon dinosaurs began to flash across the screen. King Kong killing the tyranosaur, the majestic Stokowski piece from *Fantasia*, 'The Lost World'.

Falken watched for a while, then turned back to his

guests. 'They ran and they swam and they fought and they flew until suddenly, quite a short time ago, really, they disappeared. Nature just gave up and started again. We weren't even apes then, just smart little rodents hiding among rocks. And when *we* go, nature will start again, with the bees, perhaps.' He walked back and sat down and picked up his pipe. 'You see, David, nature knows when to give up.'

'You say you're giving *up*?' David said. '*Why?*'

'It's funny,' Falken said. 'The whole point was to find a way to practice nuclear war without actually destroying ourselves. Let the machines learn from mistakes we couldn't afford to make. I never could get Joshua to learn the most important lesson.'

'And what's that?' David asked.

Falken stared straight at David. 'When to give up. That there's a time when you should just stop trying. Jennifer, did you ever play tic-tac-toe? As a child?'

'Sure,' Jennifer said. 'Everybody does.'

'But you don't any more. Why?'

'I don't know, it's boring ... always a tie.'

'Unless your opponent makes a stupid mistake, there's no way to win,' Falken said, relighting his pipe. 'Joshua was mad for games, but he couldn't learn that lesson.' He sighed. 'And now that lame-brained McKittrick has all that hardware attached to him. You see, we idealize our own technology much too much. McKittrick is a case in point.'

'If you felt that way,' David said, 'why did you leave?'

Falken puffed a moment as though considering, then said, 'At first, I took refuge in the insanity of mutual assured destruction. A plan that guaranteed total devastation on both Russian and American sides. No victory, no winner, and, therefore, no reason for war. But as missiles became more accurate, they conceived of "surgical strikes", with acceptable civilian casualties rounded off to the nearest ten million.' His voice became barbed. 'The delusion arrived that there actually could be a victory ... a winner. Nuclear war became plausible, then possible, and now, probable. Feeling time was limited, I decided to leave the magic mountain. For security reasons they graciously offered me my death, and I accepted.'

Deep in thought, Falken glanced back at the TV set. A Ray Harryhausen creature moved through primeval forests.

'Did you know,' Falken said finally, 'that no land animal with a body weight greater than fifty pounds survived that age?'

'No,' David said, 'and I don't care. Call them!'

Falken studiously ignored David's demands. 'We don't really know what happened. Perhaps a great asteroid collided with the Earth or radiation poured down from an exploding supernova. In any case, it was inevitable and they were powerless to change it. Extinction is part of the natural order, it seems.'

'Wait a sec,' David said, standing up. 'If we're extinguished, that's not natural. It's just *stupid*!'

'Not to worry,' Falken said, brightening. 'I've planned ahead. We're a mere three miles from a primary target. A millisecond of brilliant light and we're vaporized. Much more fortunate than the millions who'll wander sightless through the smoldering aftermath. We'll be spared the horror of survival.'

'So you won't even make a simple phone call?'

Jennifer said, 'If the real Joshua were still alive, you'd do it!'

164

Falken looked wistful. 'We might gain a few years, perhaps time enough for *you* to have a son. But war games, the carefully planned suicide of humankind ...' Falken smiled sadly. 'I can't stop that.'

David walked over and turned off the VCR. 'We're not dinosaurs, Dr Falken. We have some free choice. Look, I admit that I was a jerk – a *real* jerk – for insisting on playing with your program. I've learned my lesson, believe me. But I didn't give up, Dr Falken. I didn't just sit there in the middle of that mountain, even though nobody listened to me. You really think you're better than McKittrick? You see, Dr Falken, futility was *my* problem too. I felt my life was futile ... and I looked to computers to give me meaning, purpose ... power. But I was wrong ... so wrong, and I realize that now. And for once, I'm trying to *do* something about it, not just sitting around feeling superior and twiddling my thumbs!'

Falken put his pipe down in an ashtray and glanced at his watch.

'You've missed the last ferry,' he said in a monotone.

'This is *unreal*!' David said. 'You know what? I think that death means nothing to you because you're dead already. What was the last thing you really cared about?'

Falken got up and stalked away. 'You may sleep on the floor, if you like.'

'You used to be a hero to me,' David shouted after him, his voice shaking with emotion. 'But now I know you're just like all the rest! You're in a loop, Falken. A regular programmed loop – and Falken ... listen, Falken!'

Falken stopped at the doorway but did not turn around.

'We're *not* computer programs, Falken!' David said force-fully. 'We're *human beings*!'

165

Falken left, and suddenly David Lightman felt despair as he had never felt it before.

On the translucent map, Soviet subs had moved closer to both East and West coasts of the United States of America. DEFCON 2 still reigned.

The battle staff in the Crystal Palace nervously monitored the inflow of strategic information as General Berringer briefed the White House on the phone on the current status.

'We have forty-eight nuclear subs closing in on the United States from these points,' he said. 'There are Soviet troops massing in East Germany and we are monitoring their bombers on alert. Ah ... sir ... I think those are rather drastic – we're just short of war already ... I know you've talked to Andropov, and he denies ... I don't know quite what is happening, Mr President ... Yes, sir, we'll keep you informed as we get new information.'

As he put down the phone, an aide holding a telex announced, 'Intelligence reports rumors of a new Soviet bomber with stealth capabilities. It can project a false radar image six hundred miles away from the real aircraft.'

'Oh, no,' Berringer said, 'they've got us chasing shadows!'

He sat down and knocked back half a small bottle of Perrier, no lime. What was it that Winston Churchill had said about the Russians? 'A riddle wrapped in a mystery inside an enigma.'

Last year his son had showed him an article from *The New Yorker* magazine by a guy named George F. Kennan. It looked at the Soviets perceptively, showing that the Soviets felt surrounded by the United States and their allies. 'Prisoners of many circumstances', the article had called them.

'Prisoners of their own past and their country's past; prisoners of the antiquated ideology to which their extreme sense of orthodoxy binds them; prisoners of the rigid system of power that has given them their authority; but prisoners, too, of certain ingrained peculiarities of the Russian statesmanship of earlier ages.'

Kennan had also noted that the Russians had '... An over-suspiciousness, a fear of being tricked or outsmarted, an exaggerated sense of prestige and an interpretation of Russia's defensive needs so extreme – so extravagant and far-reaching – that it becomes in itself a threat to the security of other nations.'

The article had brought about a real argument between Berringer and his son, and now the general wished the softheaded snot were here now to see *this*.

The friggin' Russians were nothing but warmongering, deceitful heathen.

General Jack Berringer felt a surge of excitement, realizing suddenly that ultimately all of this was inevitable, that nuclear confrontation was his destiny.

And in his heart of hearts, he thanked God that he was on the side of truth and justice.

To say nothing of the American Way.

A mean rush of wind slapped at the trees, blowing branches and leaves about, creating a whooshing background sound to David Lightman's stumble through the darkness, Jennifer Mack in tow.

'Could we slow down?' she asked. 'Can't this wait until tomorrow? Falken's rug looked awfully comfortable.'

A moon almost full broke through a cloud and illuminated

a pathway down the wooded slope, toward a steep rocky incline. Somewhere an owl hooted.

'And wake up vaporized?' David said. 'Uh uh. That's not for me. I'm going to fight. There's gotta be something more I can do.'

'I'm so tired, David. Maybe Falken's right, maybe it *is* futile.' The smell of pine needles was strong in the air, though, and it was full of a life that David had not lived fully and a life that he did not care to deny to millions of other people. 'C'mon,' he told her. 'We'll find a boat.' His eyes searched eagerly as they made their way down the rocks. 'There's got to be a boat.'

A gust of wind smacked them, full of sea and night. The tide was pouring in, surf reflected white in the moonlight, sounding its eternal crashing mantra, David ignored the bite of the chill as he scrambled along the shore, squinting desperately into the dark sea, straining to see a boat.

He stopped, angry and frustrated, after several minutes of search.

'What kind of an idiot lives on an island and doesn't even have a boat!' he cried out to the sky. Stars winked through breaks in the cloud, indifferent and remote.

Jennifer looked out over the water. 'Maybe we could swim. How far do you think it is?'

David said, 'Two, three miles at least. Maybe more.'

Jennifer's eyes were suddenly bright in the moon. 'What do you think? Let's go for it!' She kicked off her shoes and started to the water.

David caught her by her sweater. 'Uh, Jennifer . . . I . . .' She turned and looked at him. 'I can't swim,' he admitted.

Jennifer was incredulous. 'You can't *swim?*'

'Just because *you're* Wonder Woman!' David said defensively.

'What kind of an idiot grows up in Seattle and doesn't even know how to swim?'

'I never got around to it, okay? There was always going to be plenty of time.'

He turned away bitterly. It was all going *wrong*! This wasn't the way it happened in stories. Too much was going against him, after all this effort. *Haven't I done enough yet? Haven't I paid the price for my mistake?*

The sounds of night, the breaking waves, all answered like incomprehensible whispers.

He felt a hand on his shoulder: Jennifer. 'I'm . . . sorry,' she said, gently.

'Oh, Jennifer, you know it was just a game . . . I wouldn't do any . . . anything to hurt *anybody*.' Miserably, he thumped down on a rock, hands over his face.

Jennifer sat down beside him. 'I know, David . . . I mean, you saved Herman, when the rest of us just sat and watched.'

'Savior of a hamster, destroyer of the *world*!'

'Don't say that. You care . . . You didn't make that machine, Falken did. You didn't make the world the way it is. People like McKittrick and Reagan and Andropov and Hitler did. Just what did you mean by a program loop, David?' she asked, gently rubbing his back. 'I'm sorry, but I don't understand computers very well.'

David looked out at the other side of the channel, softly bathed now in moonlight. 'Well, a computer program is like . . . like a recipe, you know?'

'You mean, like chocolate cake?' Jennifer seemed to think this most amusing.

'Yeah, only in mathematics, an algorithm.'

'I know more about chocolate cakes, I think.'

'Okay, now suppose you have a machine that cooks and bakes, a robot ... but it can only do what you tell it to do. So you write down the directions in the order they are supposed to happen – break the eggs, add the milk and flour, mix – and then you program this mechanical cook to do it. Now, suppose there is a section of the recipe in which you have to repeat a process – the directions in the recipe would tell the robot to go back to sentence number eight of the recipe and do it over again. But if you don't include a direction to go on with things, the robot will just keep repeating, breaking the eggs, adding the milk and flour, mixing, over and over again ... and never get to turning on the oven and baking the cake. That's the best example I can come up with now. Just think of that poor robot with junk all over the kitchen, endlessly adding and mixing. That's a loop, Jennifer.'

'I see! You mean, like a neurosis!' she said.

'Huh?'

'Like, even though I know I've locked the house door, I sometimes go back a couple of times to check, because I know I forget sometimes. A loop of behavior!'

'Well, I'm not so sure about that ...'

'What you said about Falken ... he's like everyone else. They're all in loops, like the robot cook.'

'Yeah, like Joshua. Joshua is just doing what he's been told to do in an endless loop. Joshua hadn't *learned* what war means and how he is involved in it,' David said. 'I have, though,' he concluded glumly.

'So what you're saying is that everyone has these loops in their behavior, the way they see things, and if they could just learn to stop it with the eggs and milk, they could go on and bake the cake.'

'Yeah, especially if the eggs and milk and flour are eventually gonna blow up the whole *world*!'

They were silent for a while, then David said, 'I wish I didn't know about any of this. I wish I was like everybody else in the world. And then, tomorrow, it would just ... be over.' He sighed. 'Then tomorrow there wouldn't be time to be sorry or guilty or whatever – about anything.' He looked across the expanse of water. 'But Jesus, I did want to learn how to swim. I swear to God I did.'

Jennifer leaned her head against his shoulder. 'Next week ...' she began. 'Next week I was going to be on TV.'

David said, 'You're kidding!'

'Oh, just on that aerobics show in the afternoon, with some of the girls in my class. Stupid, I guess. I mean, nobody'd be watching anyway.'

'I would,' David said, and he meant it.

She smiled, and David looked into her eyes, seeing how they reflected the moonlight, and thought that he'd never seen anything more beautiful in his whole life. A warmth spread through him, a gentle tingle at first and then a rush, and suddenly he was completely lost in her beauty.

'I don't want to die,' he found himself saying, and then her lips were against his and nothing had ever seemed more *right* to him in his life. Her freshness, her smell, her gentleness, her eagerness for touch, seemed to flow through him, connecting one place to another place, coursing to areas of himself and his awareness he hadn't even known he had.

When they paused for a hurried breath, David said, 'I never kissed a girl and meant it before today, Jennifer.'

171

She answered not with words but with a smile and a tug. He melted into her on the ground, and suddenly the sea and the stars were gone, and her hair and body and warm mouth were the whole universe.

A universe that knew nothing of computers or programs or missiles or bombs . . . only life and wonder.

The stars were turned on again. The sea made its sounds.

David Lightman felt a peace and purpose he'd never known before as he hurried along the rocky shoreline, the scent, the feel of Jennifer still clinging to him, Jennifer herself not far behind.

'There's gotta be *something* around here!' David said, repeating himself.

'Lots of water, for sure!' Jennifer said.

David crawled over a jumble of rocks. Spray slapped against him. 'Hey,' he yelled. 'Over here. Looks like a boat!'

The outlines of a skiff's prow jutted above the waterline, connected to a pole on the shore by a rope.

David scampered down and started pulling it in. Jennifer hurried to help him. Together they managed to tug the small vessel ashore.

They were so engrossed in their work, they did not hear the *thup-thup* sound of the helicopter in the distance.

Jennifer looked down at the boat. 'David, it's full of *water!*'

'God, I hope it just capsized and there's no hole in it,' David said, casting about for a solution. He spied a nearby pile of junk. Could there be some kind of pail in that mess? It was worth a try.

As he fished through the tattered rope, nets, and broken

172

wood, he heard the helicopter sound, but did not recognize it. 'What's that?'

'What's what?' Jennifer responded. 'I don't hear anything but the roar of the wind.'

David shrugged and went back to work, Jennifer joining in. 'Hey,' said David, 'we might be able to use this. Help me pull –'

The sound thundered over them this time, emerging from the crest of the trees. A spear of light swung through the air, slashing through the dimness in a sweeping search.

They were both frozen and blinded as the light found them, and the helicopter swooped straight toward them, rotors flashing in the reflected light.

'Let's get *out* of here!' David cried, grabbing Jennifer by the arm and pulling her behind him. They stumbled over the rubble and a collection of strewn driftwood.

The chopper pursued them like some maddened giant insect of the night.

David tripped and fell into the wet sand, bringing Jennifer down with him. The machine swooped over their heads, sending up a huge cloud of windblown sand.

David was so furious, he was almost in tears. 'The traitor turned us in!'

The helicopter turned around.

'It's coming back for us!' Jennifer screamed.

What was it going to do, David wondered as he desperately picked himself up, strafe them?

But as he helped Jennifer to her feet, the helicopter stopped, hovering in the air for a moment. Then it drifted slowly, ominously toward them.

And landed, gently, kicking up more sand.

'I say,' came a voice from the side of the cockpit. An interior light illumined the face of Dr Stephen Falken. 'Do you two fancy a rather exotic game of life and death? I believe it's *our* move now.'

David turned to Jennifer. 'He made the call.'

Jennifer whooped joyfully, and they ran toward the waiting helicopter. Falken helped them in.

'Rather fancied one last flight before I cashed in my chips,' Falken said with a smile.

'What did they say?' David asked as the rotors picked up speed.

'Oh, they were rather astonished to hear from me, and were delighted at the thought of having you back, but they seemed *awfully* preoccupied with other things! I tried to tell them what was happening, but the lovely folks wouldn't believe me. McKittrick included. So I'm afraid we're going to have to make a little visit.'

'Okay!' said David, grabbing on to the proffered shred of hope and grasping Jennifer's hand as the helicopter lifted from the island and headed east.

Chapter Ten

Riding at an altitude of twenty-two thousand miles, sentinels of war and peace, hang the most important United States missile attack warning satellites of the Defense Support Program (DSP). Their orbits are synchronous – they travel in stationary equatorial orbits, maintaining the same position, the same constant vantage point. One satellite in the eastern hemisphere keeps track of launches from Soviet and Chinese territory. Two western hemisphere satellites detect SLBM launches from the Atlantic and Pacific oceans. These items of technology scan their assignments every ten seconds, seeking the telltale strong infra-red signals from rocket plumes behind missile boosters. Earth-based computers can then plot the general direction of flight of the missiles from this information.

Backing up this system is the Ballistic Missile Early Warning System (BMEWS) radar stations in England, Alaska, and Greenland, to detect the incoming ICBMs and estimate landing points. The PAVEPAWS radar stations on the East and West coasts of the United States watch for Submarine Launched Ballistic Missiles.

The DSP satellites give twenty-five minutes of warning for

an ICBM attack and seven to ten minutes' warning for an SLBM attack.

In the Crystal Palace, deep in the heart of Cheyenne Mountain, Colorado, a claxon suddenly shattered the tense silence of the technicians.

'We have a launch detection,' a bodiless voice said over a loudspeaker. 'We have a launch detection!'

A map of the Soviet Union suddenly flashed onto one of the array of screens. A multitude of missile launches appeared, scattered through the Russian heartland.

The battle floor instantly erupted into frenzied activity.

'BMEWS has confirmed a massive attack,' a voice announced.

Another voice overlapped: 'Missile warning. *No* malfunction.'

Someone said, 'Confidence is high, I repeat, confidence is high!'

'Negative,' said another voice. 'This is not an exercise, Cobra Dane.'

John McKittrick stood in the command balcony, feeling helpless and impotent, watching the deadly events unfold.

Though it was early morning outside, eternal twilight reigned in the Crystal Palace. McKittrick had been up most of the night with Berringer, working with the machines. Deep in his gut, desperation was slowly turning to fear.

General Berringer still rode command staunchly despite his own lack of sleep. He watched the Soviet map with a grim but cynical acceptance as Captain Newt turned to him to say, 'General, DSP is tracking three hundred inbound ICBMs.'

Berringer shot a look at McKittrick that was easily equal to the power of several megaton missiles. 'Tell me this is

176

one of your simulations!' he shouted at the computer expert.

McKittrick flinched, then wearily shook his head. 'Jack, I wish I could. No one's running anything down there.'

Berringer swung toward Colonel Conley manning the communications chair. 'You better flush the bombers and get the subs ready. We're at DEFCON 1. Right now.'

McKittrick looked up at the scoreboard. It changed to DEFCON 1, and although his lover, Pat Healy, was nearby, he did not think of her now, nor did he think of himself. He thought of Randy and Allen, junior high school students even now rousting themselves out of bed to catch their buses on time, and he thought of Elinor fixing oatmeal or scrambling eggs and fixing bag lunches, and a terrible pang of regret shot through him.

He tried to allow his professionalism to push away the dread, the anticipated grief, the helplessness, but even that failed. Unaccountably, an image intruded upon his mind: sitting with his sons, watching TV in the living room. Nothing special, just a remembrance of tranquility, of calm happiness, just a wave of satisfaction flowing through his mind – something peculiar in a life generally so fraught with dissatisfaction. It was dissatisfaction with his wife that had thrown him into the arms of a younger woman. Dissatisfaction with the system had driven him to attempt to improve it, single-handedly. Dissatisfaction with life itself had driven him to search for power through his machines – to build a world where he was king and sorcerer.

And now, missiles from a foreign land were arching toward him to smash his dreams, to obliterate even the smallest satisfaction, to start the nuclear chain reactions that would destroy them all.

John McKittrick fidgeted, fighting for control of his breath. *Duty*, he thought. *I must concentrate on my duty.*

He moved over behind the WOPR terminal. Major Lem was manning it now, his balding head gleaming in the strip light, his face dotted with moisture, the odor of perspiration and Right Guard pervasive throughout the area. His delicate hands were clenched into fists as he stared at the terminal screen.

'What have we got, Major?' Berringer barked tersely.

'Just a moment, sir. I've already queried,' returned Major Lem, staring resolutely at the screen. McKittrick noticed the remains of a torn styrofoam cup by the rollers of the major's chair. 'It's coming, sir, just a moment.'

The screen's cursor left a trail of white letters over the green background. Major Lem read, somehow keeping the quiver that was in his face and neck from showing in his voice: 'Initial attack profile: massive Soviet counterforce strike. Anticipated losses: eighty-five to ninety-five per cent of our land-based strategic forces.'

General Berringer closed his eyes in a moment of obvious pain. His voice was dry. 'What does the WOPR recommend, Major?'

On a larger screen of the War Operations board, a map of the Soviet Union appeared, littered with Xs.

Lem hit a button, and the readout screen wiped. New letters quickly took its place.

'Full-scale retaliatory strike, sir, concentrated on enemy command, strategic, and industrial targets,' Lem reported.

'I need a machine to tell me that?' Berringer said.

McKittrick noticed Colonel Conley in his communications position, swiveling around. The chair squeaked.

'Sir,' he said to General Berringer, 'the President is on his way to Andrews to join Airborne Command. Sir, we've got to give him a launch option.' Conley's eyes were wide and bloodshot and nervous.

Berringer said, 'Has he been in contact with the Premier?'

'Yes, sir,' Conley said. 'The Soviets continue to deny everything.'

Berringer looked at McKittrick, and suddenly McKittrick felt a wave of compassion for the man. Here he was in a position of incredible responsibility – a position of power that he had fought and bullied his way up the ranks for through decades of military service – at a moment of supreme national importance. And it was clear from the look on his face that General Jack Berringer would rather be somewhere else. He looked suddenly like an old man.

A voice blared from the PA. 'No submarine launch detection as yet . . . Monitoring.'

McKittrick watched as Berringer gazed hopelessly at the big board, at the missiles nearing their country, at the gathering submarines off the coastline, pregnant with death.

'Let's go into a launch mode,' he said. 'Close up the mountain.'

David Lightman had experienced twinges of airsickness in the rough flight in the Air Force plane from Oregon, and now he felt more than a little carsick in the back of the Air Force jeep racing and jouncing its way toward Cheyenne Mountain. He sat in the backseat with Jennifer, while Falken, in a jolly mood, sat next to Sergeant Jim Travis, the driver.

The wind buffeted the canvas top of the jeep as it advanced

179

through steep meadowland. Snowcapped peaks stuck up before them, craggy and dark.

'Majestic!' Falken cried, exuberantly. 'In my island retreat I had forgotten the delights of the Rocky Mountains. Proud, beautiful, and virtually uninhabitable!'

'Ah'm from Louisiana, sir,' said Travis, 'and I do know what you mean.' Jim Travis was a lanky, short-haired man whose eyes sparkled with enthusiasm when he worked the gearshift of the jeep – which he did much too often for David's taste.

'How can you sit and admire the scenery at a time like this,' Jennifer said, peering past Travis, as though searching for their destination.

'Got the pedal on the floorboard, ma'am,' Travis drawled. 'Goin' 'bout as fast as we can go right now.'

'Thank God it's a nice day,' David muttered.

'Oh, yes,' said Falken, 'and I can hear the dear old President ending his Hot Line chat with Andropov ... "Have a nice day, Premier."'

Falken had been this way the whole trip – bright and cheery, full of jokes. 'My dear boy,' he had said to David, 'this is merely my particular brand of sheer lunatic *panic*.' But even that was said with a grin.

'We're there!' Jennifer said, pointing toward the complex of buildings and parking lots up ahead. 'We're there!'

David looked through the windshield, over Falken's slumped shoulder. As the jeep rounded a curb, an Air Force truck barreled toward them. The truck slowed to a stop, blocking the road. David could see other signs of activity past the truck: vehicles moving, troops running, pedestrians scattering.

180

A mustached airman pushed open a door of the truck and hopped to the ground, running toward them, gesturing frantically.

'Hey, go back. Everybody's got to divert to shelter area four,' he yelled, pointing. 'There's something really strange going on!'

Travis got out of the jeep. 'These men are on top priority. I'm taking them to NORAD command.'

'No way, Sergeant,' the airman said, shaking his head. 'Barricades are up on the main road and they're gonna button up the mountain.'

David had long since forgotten his car sickness. He watched as the airman jumped back into his truck and began to head for the designated shelter. Sergeant Travis vaulted back into the jeep.

'Looks like a bit of a *do*!' Falken said, for the first time an edge creeping into his voice.

'You think . . .' said Jennifer, 'you think they're starting the war?'

David said desperately, 'Can't we go *around* the barricades . . . or *through* them?'

A good-ole-boy grin stole over Sergeant Travis's face. 'We can sure as hell try. We ain't the Dukes of Hazzard, and this thang ain't the General Lee – but then, the General Lee ain't got four-wheel drive!'

He shifted into first, and left a rooster tail of dust behind as he peeled out, pulling off the road and racing down a steep embankment.

For once, Stephen Falken had nothing to say. He hung on to his seat belt with one hand and braced himself, his face blanching. Jennifer grabbed hold of David, clinging for dear life. David managed to get knees and hands between himself and the front seat, thus bracing himself so that he only bounced a little.

'Whoooeeee!' Travis yelped, knuckles white on the steering wheel. 'These thangs sure do move if you let 'em off their leash!'

The jeep seemed to gallop through a meadow, tearing up grass and dandelions, jouncing and shaking him so much that David couldn't make out what was ahead of them: a sea of green or an expanse of blue sky. Soon, it was all just a blue-green blur.

'You're choking me, Jennifer!' he objected, gasping.

'Sorry,' she said, but did not let go her panicked grasp until the jeep seemed to level out.

Suddenly the vehicle tilted at an incredible angle.

'Did we take *off*?' Jennifer wanted to know, her eyes clenched shut.

'Not yet,' answered David. 'But it looks like – '

They climbed a steep embankment, Sergeant Travis shifting gears like a madman, a manic grin still plastered on his face.

David was peering through the windshield. Up ahead was the crest of a ridge.

'Travis! Travis, slow down!' Falken said.

'Geronimo!' cried Sergeant Travis as his jeep seemed to grow booster rockets in its rear, its engine growling as it leaped over the ridge.

David heard a scream and, with a shock of surprise, realized that it was his own.

Inside the Crystal Palace, Lieutenant Rick Haldeman put

down the phone and turned to his assistant, Sergeant Ed Rodrigues.

'It's a go,' the curly-haired lieutenant said grimly.

'Whew, I hope it's just a precaution,' the sergeant said, getting out his checklist and handing it to the lieutenant. He swiveled back to face the bank of monitors, each show-ing different views of the surrounding area and approach-ing roads. His hands hovered over a field of buttons and switches.

'Well, precaution or the real thing, the general says to seal Cheyenne Mountain, so let's *do* it, Sarge.'

'Right.'

'Initiate internal power.'

Sergeant Rodrigues's hand deftly flicked the proper switches, tapped the proper buttons. Then he checked his meters. 'Generators on and functioning.'

'Disconnect external power . . .'

A few more switches, a few more buttons, a query from a readout screen, an override, and it was done. 'External power disconnected.'

'Seal off ventilation shafts . . .'

'Shaft locks sealed,' Rodrigues said. His eyes flicked again over the monitors, catching movement in one of them, which showed the outside access road.

Something was coming up over the ridge, fast.

My God, it's a jeep!

It leaped over the embankment, landed hard, and zoomed toward the gate.

'Sir, there's someone trying to make the entrance,' Ser-geant Rodrigues said.

The lieutenant did not even look. 'You know the rules.

We've drilled on this before, Sergeant. Now continue sealing procedures.'

'Yes, sir,' said Rodrigues, and he continued flicking switches just as the lieutenant ordered.

The jeep slammed onto the road, hard, jolting David Lightman out of place, nearly sending him and Jennifer Mack sailing over the seat into Stephen Falken's lap.

Sergeant Travis struggled for control of the wheel. The car slewed back and forth on the road, then straightened.

'Yahooooooo!' Travis yelped, gunning the engine, speedshifting the gears. 'Now all we got to do is to deal with the gate!'

David hoisted his head up, disentangling himself from a dazed Jennifer. Through the windshield he saw up ahead a wide expanse of gate.

A closed gate.

He waited for Sergeant Travis to slow down, but Travis's right foot showed no sign of straying from its position, clamped hard onto the floorboard.

'Get down and brace yourselves!' Travis commanded.

The gate approached, loomed, and then seemed to be all around them like a net, as the jeep crashed through with a scream of torn metal.

'We *did* it!' Travis cried. But no sooner had the words left his mouth than he lost his grip on the steering wheel. The vehicle veered out of control, skidding around. The surroundings seemed to swirl about David Lightman's head. The next thing he knew, the jeep was on its side and Jennifer was sprawled over him.

The canvas roof had torn off. Falken and Travis were in

a tangled heap a couple feet away, struggling to separate themselves. David picked himself up and helped Jennifer to her feet. She seemed woozy, but definitely conscious. 'Are you okay?' he asked.

'Yeah, I think so,' she answered.

'How about you guys?' He turned to Travis and Falken.

'This don't happen to Duke Wayne!' Travis said, mortified.

'Well, I do believe that is the way,' Falken said, pointing to the tunnel entrance. 'Let's go before the idiots close it!'

They raced on foot to the tunnel. 'Hurry up!' Jennifer called, running well ahead of them, David and the others puffing behind. 'There's a big door up there ... and it's starting to close!'

Stephen Falken opened his mouth as though thinking about emitting a witticism, but apparently decided to save his energy for the dash.

Their footsteps echoed around them as they entered the tunnel. David Lightman looked up and saw what Jennifer had seen: The thick blast door at the end of the tunnel, seemingly miles distant, was beginning to close.

'We got thirty seconds!' Sergeant Travis yelled.

David Lightman suddenly wished he had exercised more.

Chapter Eleven

In November 1979 a NORAD technician accidentally fed the wrong tape into the main computers.

Not realizing that they were watching a computer war game, NORAD commanders observed a classic nuclear attack pattern developing on their display screens, with Soviet missiles headed straight for SAC bomber bases. So real seemed the alert that the President's command jet took off before the generals realized what was going on.

In June 1980 a faulty microchip worth perhaps forty-six cents created a series of ghost attacks on the boards.

General Jack Berringer had been in charge of NORAD then, and he had made certain with the help of John McKittrick's staff that there were plenty of backup systems to detect just such faulty warnings.

All of these systems agreed with the boards now: the United States was being attacked by Soviet missiles.

There could be no doubt of that.

Berringer watched as his battle staff prepared for the upcoming combat conditions, notifying the various civilian and military defense posts throughout the world by phone and radio.

Major Lem turned to Berringer from his control board. 'All wings report missiles targeted and enabled, awaiting launch codes.'

'We are in a launch mode,' came Colonel Conley's voice over the loudspeaker.

Berringer turned to Major Lem and said, 'Lock out changes.'

Lem leaned over his terminal and began to type in the instructions.

Jack Berringer had suppressed all feeling by now. He was pure action, pure adrenaline, pure duty.

He watched as his people and his machines worked in their deadly symbiosis; watched as the screen spelled out the obvious:

MISSILES TARGETED AND ENABLED.
CHANGES LOCKED OUT.

When the call had come last night from Dr Stephen Falken, Patricia Healy had been on the command balcony, aiding the WOPR monitor, and John McKittrick had been down with his machines.

In lieu of McKittrick, she had been put on the line.

'Hullo, John, I hear you've a bit of a mess over there,' the British-accented voice had said.

'I'm sorry, this isn't Dr McKittrick, this is his assistant, Patricia Healy,' she said in measured tones. Finally she was talking to the infamous Falken. 'I'm afraid Dr McKittrick is busy with the computers.'

'Ah, just thought I'd give a ring from the dead. Only a few folks know I'm still kicking about. As you express no shock, I suppose you're one of them,' the voice went on. 'Now then, since I can't reach John, perhaps you'd better give me General Zeppelin or Berlitzer or whatever his name is.'

'I'll see what I can do,' she had answered. It took some convincing, but Pat finally got the fatigued commander onto the phone. 'Falken!' the man said gruffly. 'Thought you were dead ... Can't talk, we have a ticklish ... What? ... Well, bring the little monster in.' Long pause. 'I find that very difficult to believe, sir. McKittrick assures us that this is not a simulation, and he's been working on these machines a lot longer than you have.' Pause. 'Look, fella, I don't care if you *did* create the Joshua program, we're dealing with the Russians now, so if you'll excuse me, I have to get to work.'

The phone had been handed back brusquely to Pat, and she had to deal with Falken.

'My goodness, a very dense fellow,' Falken had said. 'Now then, maybe you can help me, Patricia. I believe what you are now observing on your boards is a continued war game. Joshua always fancied himself quite the Napoleon and –'

'Wait. I've been through the readouts ... we even did work on the CPUs, Falken,' she said. 'John ... I mean, Dr McKittrick is the finest mind presently working on defense computers in the world, and he can find no indication of any faulty operation in our computer system.'

'Oh that McKittrick was always the nitwit,' Falken said. 'Look, I can see there's no good in talking to you; apparently I'm going to have to zip off for Colorado myself, so could you have the grace to inform John of my imminent arrival and could you please prepare our security clearance – that's for myself and a very persistent pair of teenagers. It would be rather a shame to go for the best seat for End of the World, and find yourself without a ticket. There's a good girl; now if you'll excuse me, I'm going to call in a few favors from the United States Air Force.'

Now Patricia Healy stood by the huge blast door, waiting for Falken's arrival. The sealing orders had just come over the loudspeakers, and where *was* Falken, anyway?

'Hurry!' she said under her breath. 'Hurry, dammit!'

She'd given Falken's call a lot of thought during the sleepless night.

When she'd told McKittrick about it, he had only sighed.

'I wish it were so, but there's no indication of a simulation this time, Pat, you know that.' Then his dark eyes had narrowed. 'You don't suppose that Falken himself has sold out to the Russians?' McKittrick grunted. 'You don't know what a few years will do for a man, do you?'

And that was that. McKittrick had refused to talk about the subject any further.

Damn, he could be *so* bullheaded sometimes! Pat had wanted to scream and pound his head, but she was just too weary. If Falken was right, he'd be able to prove it. But first he'd have to get here.

So Patricia Healy, in her rumpled skirt and smeared make-up, gazed hopefully up the entrance tunnel to the Crystal Palace. No sign of Falken, whatsoever. From the way McKittrick talked about Falken, he seemed almost mythological. The man had laid much of the groundwork for the computer net here at NORAD – architect of the Holy of Holies in the pantheon of John McKittrick. A puckish deity, head in Olympian clouds most of the time. But the exile was returning home now. To save the day? *Hard to say*, Patricia Healy thought, but at this point she was willing to grasp hold of any shred of hope.

From what she had heard of him, and from the evidence of her studies of the computer system he had set up, if there was any hope, it rested with Falken. He had created the WOPR – a program so advanced that at times Patricia Healy had almost considered it intelligent.

John McKittrick insisted that someone from *outside* had tampered with the program, creating the problems – all part of a Russian scheme. The proud man would not admit the possibility that Falken was right; that somehow his program – which he called 'Joshua' – was playing World War III for real.

So if there was anyone now who could convince General Jack Berringer of this possibility, it was Dr Stephen Falken.

But where *was* he?

A pair of guards stood by the door, each wearing the look of stunned professionalism peculiar to the career soldier in combat.

The first of the massive blast doors, more than three feet thick and with a swing weight of twenty-five tons encased in a concrete collar, was beginning to close.

'We better get ready to move on, ma'am,' one of the guards, a slim, handsome blond fellow, said, anxiously eyeing the other blast door fifty feet away, which would close next.

'We've got thirty seconds,' Pat Healy said.

'Oh yeah,' the other guard, a corporal, said. 'Lots of time!'

Desperately, Patricia Healy turned back to the tunnel, hoping against hope that Falken and company would make it, realizing that it was now most likely they would not and –

Suddenly there were four figures running toward the door, their steps echoing through the tunnel.

'Folks you been waitin' for, ma'am?' the corporal asked.

'Pray to God they are!' Pat Healy said.

'Ma'am, I been prayin' for a couple of days straight.'

'Amen!' said the other guard.

The hydraulics of the blast door hissed away the seconds.

At the forefront of the party was a young girl, sprinting like an athlete, yards ahead of her companions. Trailing her was an Air Force sergeant; then came that boy, David Lightman; and finally a tall, loping older man –

Dr Stephen Falken!

'They're going to make it!' she said joyfully.

'Yeah, with a healthy five seconds to spare!' said the guard, getting out of the way as Jennifer Mack charged through the narrowing space between blast door and collar. The others were right behind her, Falken barely making it as the heavy door clunked shut.

'They're cleared . . . they're cleared!' Patricia Healy said.

'Well, we can't kick 'em back out now, that's for sure,' said the guard. 'C'mon, we gotta get through that other door, folks.'

'I say,' Falken puffed. '*Chariots of Fire* stuff, eh?'

'I'm Patricia Healy,' Pat said as she ran with the party to the next blast door, which was already beginning to close. 'I'm Dr McKittrick's assistant, and I presume that you're Stephen Falken.'

'He is! He is!' David Lightman said.

'Oh dear, my cover is blown,' said Falken. 'Do not ask for Hume the Bell Tolls!'

Feeling as though his lungs were on fire, David Lightman followed Patricia Healy through the double doors leading into the Crystal Palace.

191

The place was a madhouse.

Despite the fact that the actual temperature had not risen, David could see droplets of sweat formed on the brows of technicians. He could almost smell the fear as machine sounds and human voices bounced about like static. Engineers and technicians dashed back and forth between stations, while others leaned over their consoles, tension creased on their faces. Others simply looked up at the big board, straining to keep the horror from their eyes.

Patricia Healy separated herself from the others and rushed up to the command balcony. Falken halted, gazing around the command center, then glanced up at the global automated battlefield he had helped to create.

David looked up at the board, and felt Jennifer's hand urgently gripping his arm. 'Oh, dear God, David. Look at that!'

The big board was glowing, brilliant and rainbow-strewn with the blipping lights of incoming Russian ICBMs.

David could hear a dim voice saying, 'DSP is still tracking three hundred inbound ICBMs presently MIRV-ing to approximately two thousand four hundred impact points.'

David Lightman felt as though he stood at the heart of a vast computer, at the very core of a mesh of humanity and machine. Standing here with the man who had made such an operation possible should have swept him up in intellectual awe – but now, considering the circumstances, he was riven with instinctual anxiety.

'I do believe that we're here, as the saying goes, in the nick of time, David,' Falken murmured.

A loud, irate voice cut through David Lightman's reverie.
'Stephen!'

David turned, immediately aware of the physical presence of John McKittrick storming toward them. McKittrick's eyes were sunken, his hair tousled. The man's looks defined the word *haggard*.

'Stephen,' McKittrick continued, drawing up even with them. 'I don't know what the hell you think you're gonna be able to do here ...'

There was a defensiveness to the man's belligerence that had all the earmarks of a grown pupil confronted by his master.

'John!' Falken smiled faintly, his hands thrust in the pockets of his gray cardigan. 'How good to see you.' He eyed the top of McKittrick's rumpled blue dress shirt. 'I see the wife still picks your ties.'

McKittrick flustered. His eyes narrowed as he glanced down at David Lightman. *If looks could kill*, thought David.

'Look,' McKittrick said, 'I don't know what this kid has told you ...'

'It's all a bluff, John,' Falken said, making an airy gesture to the big board as though it were nothing.

McKittrick blinked. 'This is *not* a bluff, dammit! This is *real*!' His face reddened. 'Everything is ready for the President to order a counterstrike, and we're advising him to do it *immediately*.'

Stephen Falken shook his head, gave McKittrick one disparaging glance, then brushed past his former assistant, heading for a point on the floor just below the command balcony.

'Hello up there!' he called.

When he got no response, Falken cupped his hands to improvise a megaphone and yelled, 'I say, hello General Jack

Berringer. Could you lend an ear? I need only a few seconds of your time.'

Falken's quite theatrical baritone attracted attention.

General Berringer stood and made his way to the lip of the balcony.

'"But, soft! What light through yonder window ..."' Falken said to McKittrick and David, then straightened up as Berringer scowled down at him.

'Falken! Well, you picked a hell of a day to visit!' Berringer growled, basso profundo.

'General, please, in all seriousness.' Falken pointed to the brilliantly lit map depicting the commencement of Armageddon. 'General, what you see on those screens up there is *fantasy*! A computer-enhanced *hallucination*! Those blips are not real missiles. They are phantoms!'

Berringer stared down silently at the party on the floor below him.

'I say, John, did the old boy inherit Brezhnev's eyebrows?' Falken asked.

'Jack,' said McKittrick, 'I have absolutely no indication of a simulation run!'

'Believe me, dammit!' Falken said, losing his humor. 'I know my program ... it all follows ... makes sense. Joshua has developed to the point where he could *do* this!'

'Two minutes to impact!' cried out an airman to General Berringer.

Throat dry, desperate, David ran up alongside Falken and called up to Berringer. 'General, your system is trying to bluff you. It's trying to get you to launch an attack because it can't launch one of its own!'

Jennifer stepped up to David and grabbed his hand.

Berringer was called away by one of his aides to a switchboard. 'Sir! Airborne Command.'

Berringer grabbed the proffered phone, but did not answer it. Instead, he shot an inquiring glance down to McKittrick, as though to ask, *Could this be possible?*

McKittrick said, 'Like I told you before, Jack, we've checked and rechecked everything. And everything in our computers is working perfectly!'

Falken stepped to a position that neatly upstaged his former assistant. 'But General, think! Does it make any sense?'

Berringer was clearly perplexed. 'Does *what* make any sense?'

Falken thrust a forefinger toward the main board. 'That, for God's sake! General, are you prepared to destroy the enemy?'

Berringer stiffened, as though about to salute an invisible American flag. 'Yes. Fully.'

'Do you think they know that?' Falken asked.

Berringer barked a sarcastic laugh. 'I believe we've made it about as clear as we could.'

'Don't fire any of your half-cocked missiles until you're *sure* that the Russians have fired theirs! Tell the President to ride out the first bit of attack ... and then, if it's real, by God, you can nuke the Russkies all you want!'

'Ninety seconds!' a voice reported.

'Sir!' a voice nagged at General Berringer. 'They need a decision.'

Falken continued, emphatically and convincingly. 'General. Do you really *believe* that the enemy would attack without provocation, with so many missiles, bombers, and subs so we would have no choice but to totally annihilate them? General, you are listening to a *machine*! Do the world a favor and don't act like one yourself!'

General Jack Berringer stared at the swarm of warhead missiles moving toward their targets. Troubled doubts registered on his tired face. He looked down at Falken, his gaze shifting to David.

David Lightman felt like going down on his knees, begging. But instead he held onto Jennifer tightly, and met General Berringer's eyes for a full, pleading second.

Berringer broke the eyelock. He picked up the phone and answered.

'Yes, Mr President,' he said, and there was the longest moment that David Lightman had ever experienced as the President spoke to the general on the other end of the line.

'Sir,' said General Berringer, looking back down at Falken. 'At this point in time I cannot positively confirm the inbounds. There's reason to believe they may not exist.'

As Berringer listened to the general's response, David released his breath in a sigh. He had not even realized that he'd been holding it. Jennifer buried her head on his chest. Her hold on him relaxed.

'Yes, sir,' Berringer continued. 'That's affirmative. Yes, sir, so do I,' he said somberly, then handed the phone back to Colonel Conley. He took a deep breath and asked, 'Who's first and how soon?'

Major Lem at the WOPR console said, 'Initial impact points – Loring Air Force Base in Maine. Three-nineteenth Bomb Wing at Grand Forks, North Dakota, and Alaskan Air Command headquarters at Elmendorf. Impacts projected in just a little over one minute, sir.'

'Get me the senior controller at each station,' Berringer ordered. 'I want to talk to them myself.' General Berringer knew that this was grasping at straws, but if they were all you had to hang on to when a big, black chasm opened up beneath you, then you grasped with all your might.

Colonel Conley's chair squeaked as he swiveled back into operation position, punching up the various command posts on his console panel. An alert warble sounded as three red lights blinked on.

'All stations,' the colonel said into the phone, 'this is Crystal Palace – stand by for a message from Brass Hat.'

General Berringer picked up his phone and listened for the communications response from the air bases nearest the presumed all-out Soviet ICBM attack.

The first voice came immediately. Colonel Conley had patched it into the loudspeaker system so that everyone could hear.

'Elmendorf Air Force Base, Operations, Lieutenant Colonel Bowers,' the voice said.

Another voice followed on its heels. 'Three-nineteenth Bomb Wing, Operations, Colonel Chase.'

The last voice had a quavering, adolescent quality. 'Uh ... this is Loring Air Force Base, uh, the senior controller isn't here right now.'

'That's all right,' Berringer said, smiling despite himself. 'Who are you?'

'Sir, this is Airman Doughterty, sir.'

'This is General Berringer of NORAD. The current situation ...' He cleared his voice and started again. 'We are tracking approximately twenty-four hundred inbound Soviet warheads ... however, at this time, we cannot confirm this.

I repeat, we *cannot confirm* this. We're estimating impact at –'

He glanced over at Airman Fields, the unofficial time-keeper, who promptly piped up, 'Twenty-five seconds, sir.'

On the other end of one of the lines, Airman Kenneth Doughterty was suddenly aware of moisture creeping down his legs.

He looked down in horror to realize that he'd wet his pants.

Lieutenant Colonel Bowers in Grand Forks figured it was just a test, so he stayed perfectly cool.

Colonel Chase, however, knew that everything was for real, and he quietly made peace with his Creator.

'We're right there with you guys,' General Berringer's voice said over all three lines. 'We've taken all the steps we can. Stand by to launch missiles on my command.'

To his added shame, Airman Doughterty realized that he was whimpering.

Berringer said, 'Stay on this channel as long as possible. We'll be standing by.'

And God help you, the General thought as a deathly stillness settled over the entire combat operations center.

Somehow the hope that Falken was right made the situation even more hellish. A man resigned to the worst prepared himself; the same doomed man, given a sliver of hope, could go mad.

Airman Fields interrupted the breathless silence to provide an unrequested countdown.

'Six seconds, sir,' the young man said, straining to keep his voice even. 'Five . . .'

All heads were turned toward the center board.

'Four . . .'

On the board above, the arcs of the leading warheads approached their targets, just about to impact on the stations at Loring, Grand Forks, and at Elmendorf.

'Three . . .'

General Berringer looked down at David Lightman and Stephen Falken. *The odd couple*, he thought.

'I hope that you're right,' he said, almost to himself.

'Two . . . one . . .'

The lights struck their targets. A spray of colored diodes splashed out designation of symbolic explosions.

'Zero,' said Airman Fields.

General Berringer grimaced. He waited for a moment, then, face pale, he nodded to Colonel Conley.

'This is Crystal Palace,' said Colonel Conley into the mouthpiece. 'Are you still there . . . I mean, are you still on? Crystal Palace, calling. Come in!'

Dead silence from the loudspeakers.

Colonel Conley's voice broke. 'This is Crystal Palace, are you still there? Come in, for God's sake.'

A burst of static fell from the speakers, followed by a voice.

'Yep,' came Lieutenant Colonel Bowers's voice. 'That's affirmative, sir.'

'Yeah, we're here,' came the squeaky voice of Airman Doughterty. 'Oh, thank God, we're still here!'

All eyes turned back to the big board, where the diodes flashed crazily with silent explosions. They looked, David Lightman thought, like a gigantic arcade game gone insane.

Colonel Conley shook his head as though to clear his vision. 'Our boards are *confirming* impact –'

'No, sir, no impact,' Colonel Chase reported. 'We're alive and well.'

A relieved General Berringer slammed a fist into his palm. 'Recall the bombers and let's stand the missiles down.'

'Oh, David, you were right!' Jennifer said, throwing her arms around him again, even as she jumped up and down with joy. David could feel the tension dissipate on the battle floor. All the technicians called out a raucous cheer.

David Lightman looked around to congratulate Falken. The man was gone.

John McKittrick was still gazing up at the board. He was obviously relieved, but nonetheless still troubled, as unanswered questions poured through his head.

'Do you believe me now?' David said. 'I really didn't mean to do it ... and I wasn't in league with anyone else.'

'I need ...' said McKittrick. 'I should talk to Falken. This Joshua ... This could be very serious ... even now.'

'Where did he go?' Jennifer asked.

McKittrick pointed.

Dr Stephen Falken was wandering along the front of the room, the huge electronics displays towering above him. He seemed oblivious to the atmosphere of celebration, as the giant map obliterated itself over and over again with its symbolic rain of nuclear explosions.

'C'mon,' David said, grabbing Jennifer by the hand, hurrying over to the computer genius. 'Falken ... Stephen ... We did it!'

'Did we?' Falken said. 'I wonder ...'

'What do you mean?' Jennifer asked.

Obviously troubled, Stephen Falken shook his head. 'Joshua won't like this. He's older now ... but he's still a child, you know, just a child who wants his way.'

On the command balcony, General Berringer and his aides

200

ebulliently congratulated themselves, while Colonel Conley ordered the bomber and submarine forces back.

Major Lem smiled as he typed instructions into the WOPR console.

His smile faded quickly as he tried to log onto the system.

What the hell! thought Major Lem, alarmed.

He turned to Colonel Conley. 'Would you get me Dr McKittrick right away?'

John McKittrick walked toward Falken. There were things that needed settling. *A lot of things*, the man thought as he made his way through the din of celebration.

Falken looked up from his conversation with David and Jennifer, and saw McKittrick approaching.

'Uh oh,' he said. 'Let's all get out of here before he offers us something to eat.'

Just as he was about to reach the group, a technician grabbed McKittrick's arm and tugged him toward a console, holding a headphone. 'Dr McKittrick,' the man said, 'Major Lem is on the line for you.'

McKittrick put on the headset.

'McKittrick here. What's up, Major?'

'Sir,' returned Major Lem's voice, 'something very strange is happening. The WOPR refuses to let me log back on. I can't get in to stand down the missiles or recall the bombers.'

I was afraid of this, thought McKittrick. He looked up, spotted Falken. 'Hold on,' he told Lem.

Quickly he sat down at a spare terminal and tapped the 'enter' key.

LOG ON, the monitor screen replied.

McKittrick tapped in:

7KQ201

McKITTRICK

The monitor responded immediately:

IDENTIFICATION NOT RECOGNIZED.
YOU HAVE BEEN DISCONNECTED.

Immediately, John McKittrick jumped up and bellowed to Falken. 'Stephen. Stephen, quickly, come here! The WOPR is not letting us back in!'

Falken hurried back to the terminal, David and Jennifer following.

McKittrick dialed up the computer center. Richter answered. 'Paul,' McKittrick said, 'I can't get into the WOPR.'

'I know,' replied Richter, a frenzied tone to his voice. 'It's weird. No one can get back on. We're trying everything. It's like the entire password file has been wiped out.'

As Stephen Falken drew up to the console where John McKittrick sat, David Lightman's attention was attracted by something on a lower screen, one below the fantasy holocaust spread out above.

A series of ten random numbers and letters flashed on the lower screen, changing so rapidly that the digits were blurred.

'Hey!' he cried, pointing up at the board. 'What are *those*?'

McKittrick shot an annoyed glance at David, but as he saw the digits, his expression changed entirely into an expression of pure dread.

'Oh, no!' McKittrick said. 'The launch codes!'

Jennifer Mack looked up at the changing numbers, then back at McKittrick. 'What are they?'

Falken pursed his lips as he looked down at the monitor screen.

'Looks like Joshua is getting ready to send up the real missiles,' he said, and there was no joking in his tone.

Chapter Twelve

As Paul Richter led a team of jumpsuited technicians through the NORAD computer center, opening up processing units, probing circuitry, frantically searching for electronic clues, to try and stop it, the computer program in the WOPR relayed its instructions to the nine ICBM missile bases located in the continental United States.

In Minutemen missile launch capsules in Montana, Utah, North Dakota, South Dakota, Kansas, Missouri, and Mississippi, identical orders played over the console display screen of the computers controlling the missiles:

MISSILES ENABLED.

TARGET SELECTION COMPLETE.

TIME ON TARGET SEQUENCE COMPLETE.

YIELD SELECTION COMPLETE.

CHANGES LOCKED OUT.

The only thing needed now to launch the missiles, snug in their silos, was the launch code.

Suddenly, at the bottom of the computer screen in all of the United States' launch capsules, ten bold white characters – three letters, four digits, three letters – appeared at the bottom changing rapidly, in seemingly random order.

There was, however, no one around to watch these numbers, anyone able to stop the launches.

For no one was inside the capsules.

And everything was now completely automatic.

David Lightman listened as Richter's voice came over the intercom.

'We've checked the random number generators, but they're not even running. I have no idea ... it could be coming from anywhere.'

'Keep looking, Paul.'

McKittrick, on the command balcony now, looked up at the confused military personnel hovering around him. 'The machine has locked us out. It's still trying to launch those missiles.'

Pat Healy was busy operating a calculator. 'There's an eighty per cent chance of it finding the bunch codes in six minutes.'

Berringer was bemused. 'For goodness sake, just unplug the stupid thing.'

Too bad Jim Sting isn't here, thought David. *He'd know what to do.*

McKittrick shook his head despairingly.

'We can't. The command capsules would interpret any shutdown to mean that this facility had been destroyed in an attack. The computers at the silos would then carry out their last instruction, which was to launch.'

Berringer fumed. 'McKittrick, after careful consideration I am prepared to tell you that your new defense system sucks!'

David watched as McKittrick lost whatever cool he had left. 'I don't have to take that ... you pig-eyed tub of rancid lard!'

'You can't even curse with originality!' Berringer said, smiling in obtuse satisfaction. 'Dimwit!'

Colonel Conley called to the general. 'Sir . . . it's the President.'

General Berringer sighed and walked to the red phone.

'What are you going to tell him?' McKittrick asked resignedly, his rage gone.

Berringer answered in a defeated voice: 'To order the bombers back to their fail-safes. We may have to go through with this after all.' His whole face seemed to sag as he accepted the phone and began to speak.

Falken turned to David and Jennifer, speaking ruminatively. 'You know, I visited a Minuteman base once upon a time. They even showed me one of the missiles. Three stages, six feet wide, seventy-eight thousand pounds. Nine megatons – oh yes, they gave me all the statistics. The one I was looking at could deliver its gift to the Russians six thousand miles away, traveling at fifteen thousand miles per hour.' He held his hand up, as though examining the ICBM again in his imagination. 'But do you know what I remember most vividly? A bit of graffiti scrawled on the fuselage of that missile. It said "Reach Out and Touch Someone".'

Falken smiled sadly and put one hand on David's shoulder. 'We've done our best.'

McKittrick was sweating over a console. He glared up at Falken. 'Stephen . . . maybe you could do it! Try and get back in, please!'

'John, I would if I could,' said Falken, holding his delicate-fingered hands up helplessly. 'But you've taken out my password. Joshua doesn't know his papa anymore!'

David was hardly aware that he was speaking, until half

the sentence was out of his mouth. 'Maybe it'll open for something it's interested in!'

'What?' McKittrick said.

'It likes to play games,' David said emphatically. 'Maybe it'll want to play a game.'

Falken shrugged and smiled as David looked at him. 'Good idea. You try it.'

'For goodness sake, Stephen –'

'No, let him,' Jennifer said. 'He's played it before. We *know* Joshua.'

Falken nodded. 'After all, he can hardly do worse than you have, John.'

David Lightman barely noticed McKittrick's reaction to the insult. He was too busy concentrating, thinking.

Okay, Lightman, he told himself. *You've put yourself on the spot. Now produce.*

Sometimes, when he got real interested in writing a program or in debugging a program, it was as though the very nature of time shifted, as though he were in some different universe altogether. Time slipped by so quickly . . . and when he 'woke up', there was something new, something he hadn't known he was capable of before.

Adding to the tension and chaos of the situation were a bunch of system programmers huddled around Major Lem at the terminal, spewing out suggestions. It sounded like the Tower of Babel!

'. . . Feed it a tapeworm,' one chubby man said.

'No, too risky,' another said. 'It might crash the system.'

'How'd the kid get in?' somebody wanted to know.

'The back door.'

'We took it out.'

'Too bad. Can we invade the deep logic?'

'We keep hitting a damn fire wall.'

Thinking hard, David watched as Major Lem tried the back-door password.

JOSHUA5

The monitor responded immediately.

IDENTIFICATION NOT RECOGNIZED.

YOU HAVE BEEN DISCONNECTED.

'There you go, old boy,' Falken said, touching David's shoulder. 'Have a go.'

'You can do it, David,' Jennifer said. 'I know you can!'

'Kid, if you can, you've got yourself a job!' McKittrick said.

David Lightman nudged his way through the huddle and leaned over Major Lem.

'Have it list games,' he suggested.

Major Lem turned back and looked at David, surprised. He turned to McKittrick with a puzzled expression.

McKittrick nodded. 'Try it, Bill.'

Jennifer said, 'No, not him. You should do it, David.'

'I guess you know it as well as I do by now,' Major Lem said, standing and allowing David to take his place.

David sat down, took a deep breath, and said a silent prayer.

He typed into the computer: GAMES.

'Put it up on the center screen, Bill,' General Berringer said, 'so we can all see it.'

Major Lem leaned over a control board and hit a few switches.

GAMES was now projected on the huge center screen of the big board.

David hit the 'return' button.

Immediately the computer reacted just as it had when David had first contacted it through his modem.

FALKEN'S MAZE

BLACKJACK

CHECKERS

CHESS

FIGHTER COMBAT

DESERT WARFARE

THEATERWIDE TACTICAL WARFARE

GLOBAL THERMONUCLEAR WAR

David Lightman typed in: CHESS.

Joshua had wanted to play chess first. Maybe he was still open for a game.

The monitor replied: IDENTIFICATION NOT RECOGNIZED.

POKER, David typed.

Maybe it was in the mood for bluffing. It certainly had been doing that enough these past few days.

But again the monitor replied: IDENTIFICATION NOT RECOGNIZED.

'Oh, no,' he said. 'The security system won't let anything through.'

'Try "Global Thermonuclear War",' Jennifer suggested.

'Okay,' David said.

He typed in GLOBAL THERMONUCLEAR WAR, to which the monitor responded: GAME ROUTINE RUNNING.

STOP GAME ROUTINE, David ordered.

There was a pause. Jennifer's nails were digging into David's shoulder, but he hardly noticed.

It seemed to take forever.

The monitor said:

IMPROPER INSTRUCTION.

ROUTINE MUST COMPLETE BEFORE RESET.

YOU HAVE BEEN DISCONNECTED.

The screen went blank.

David felt like crying. The programmers were jockeying for position, eager to try new approaches. David looked out over the balcony railing, watching the furious activity below. He glanced at Falken, then to the launch codes running out rapidly on the lower screen of the big board.

It seemed so frustrating . . .

So futile . . . so *very* futile . . . !

'Futile!' He shouted.

'Huh?' General Berringer said.

'Futile!' David Lightman cried.

'Well, if it's futile, fellow, get the hell away from there and let someone else try!' the general said.

'No, no, you don't understand. What you said before, Dr Falken! On the island!'

Quickly he turned back to the WOPR terminal and put the games list back up.

'We've already tried that!' Lem said.

'Falken, it's not on the list. Why isn't it on the list?' David asked, as the games list flashed onto the large screen.

'What?'

David typed in TIC-TAC-TOE and entered it.

Nothing happened.

'If it's not on the list, it's not in the computer, surely,' McKittrick said.

Nothing happened for a moment, then: NO SUCH PROGRAM, the monitor said.

'You were telling me that you played it with Joshua, your son, dammit!' David cried desperately. 'Where is it?'

Falken smiled. 'Oh, yes, my goodness, but that was . . . I say, you're right, David, I'd forgotten all about that program. That was an easy . . . Well, it's really quite simple.' He leaned over and typed in another word:

PLAY

. . . and then entered it by hitting the 'return' button.

'Different file, dear boy.'

Immediately the monitor responded:

SNAKE

TIC-TAC-TOE

HOPSCOTCH

David typed in: RUN TIC-TAC-TOE.

Two pairs of intersecting lines appeared on the screen.

'What the hell?' General Berringer said. 'This is not the time . . .'

'No, wait, General, I think I see what he's doing.'

ONE OR TWO PLAYERS?

PLEASE LIST NUMBER.

Joshua requested.

The tic-tac-toe grid illuminated the center screen of the big board.

'You're in!' McKittrick cried. 'Order it to disarm the missiles and cease random function immediately!'

Major Lem pushed David aside and tried to follow McKittrick's instructions.

The tic-tac-toe graphic on the board vanished, replaced by letters from Joshua:

IMPROPER INSTRUCTION.

CHANGES LOCKED OUT.

210

YOU HAVE BEEN DISCONNECTED.

The screen went blank.

'Excuse me,' said David. He typed PLAY. The new list appeared again. The tic-tac-toe game reappeared at his command.

'You're going to play it?' McKittrick asked incredulously.

'You bet I am!' David answered.

Joshua requested:

ONE OR TWO PLAYERS?

LIST NUMBER OF PLAYERS.

David typed in: ONE.

X OR O?

X GOES FIRST.

3 IN A ROW WINS.

'X in the center square!' somebody shouted up from the floor below.

'Brilliant strategy!' Falken said. 'I say, General, your chaps may have found their calling.'

'Shut up, Falken.'

David typed in: X IN CENTER SQUARE.

An O appeared immediately in a corner.

David played out the game, until all the squares were filled.

Joshua quickly announced the outcome:

STALEMATE.

WOULD YOU CARE TO PLAY AGAIN?

Someone shouted from the floor: 'You can't win!'

'I know that,' David said. 'But it hasn't learned! This computer can learn! Dr Falken says it can learn!' He turned to Falken. 'Is there any way to make it play against itself?'

'Let me see, it's been years since I programmed that game,'

said Falken, perplexed. 'Ah yes. When it asks the number of players, type in "zero".'

David obeyed.

He took a deep breath and entered his command.

On the screen an *X* appeared in the center of the grid.

A game filled up the board, *X*s shuffling after *O*s, until the inevitable stalemate. Then the *X*s and *O*s vanished, leaving a blank board. Another game began, this one a little quicker, *X* after *O* after *X*, to stalemate.

'I don't understand,' McKittrick said.

'Surely you're aware of Joshua's charm, John,' Falken said.

McKittrick's eyes widened. 'The integration program, of course.'

'What?' Berringer demanded, watching as the games began to flash faster and faster.

'Joshua is a sum total of all its programs, General,' McKittrick said, eyes glued to the screen. 'Like the human brain, it's holistic.'

'Yes, of course,' said Patricia Healy.

'I still don't understand,' General Berringer said.

'All computers have separate systems usually, only peripherally linked,' Pat answered. 'General, if you stuck your foot into something hot and got burned, would you touch it with your bare hand?'

'No, of course not.'

'But your foot is different from your hand.'

'I should hope so.'

'Your CPU ... your central processing unit ... your brain, has integrated programming too,' Pat Healy said. 'What David is trying to do is stick Joshua's foot in the fire.'

212

David was tapping the 'enter' key, as though to keep goading Joshua.

'C'mon,' he said. 'Learn, God damn it. Learn.'

Up on the screen, the battle of the Xs and Os continued on and on, faster and faster, in its flickering no-win loop.

'It sure is consuming system power!' Major Lem said, glancing at a readout. 'It's going nuts!'

The screen was just a blur now of white and black.

'The program must be playing hundreds of games a second,' McKittrick said.

Major Lem said excitedly, 'Look! The random numbers ... the launch codes are slowing down!'

The strobing lights reflected off Paul Richter's glasses. 'It's caught in a loop,' he said, amazed. 'And the loop is forcing it to draw more and more power from the rest of the system!'

The group watched breathlessly as the wildly flashing lights made the battle floor and command balcony of the Crystal Palace look more like a disco dance floor than the center of operations for a multibillion-dollar defense network.

David turned to Falken as though for encouragement.

Falken wore the slightest trace of a smile ... Which meant there was hope.

David turned back to the screen. The intensity of the dueling symbols seemed to have increased.

Suddenly there was a brilliant flash.

David and the others shielded their eyes.

The screen went dark.

'Uh oh!' David said, his hopes falling.

Giant projections of the Earth, Mercator maps, filled all twelve screens.

The light show assumed prismatic colors, dazzling the onlookers. The symbols for submarines, bombers, and missiles swarmed over the screen like electronic insects, buzzing back and forth in their crazed, kamikaze dance. World War III between the West and the East ended in a blaze of symbolic mushroom clouds and blasts, leaving huge blackened areas.

Suddenly the board was virgin again. Bombers swept across the globe in different patterns. Volleys of missiles were launched, impacting in seconds.

Again the nuclear exchange, despite different strategy, ended in the total destruction of both sides.

Berringer grabbed McKittrick's arms. 'What's it doing?'

David turned to both. 'He's learning ... Joshua's finally learning.'

The exchange commenced once more, faster. Within seconds the translucent boards were splashes of blazing colors, totally indecipherable, a mass of flashing diodes.

'A repeat of the tic-tac-toe,' said the general. 'I see ... but what difference does it make?'

Suddenly the screen flashed off. The random numbers clicked to a halt.

'Did it burn itself out?' the general demanded anxiously. 'It could still blast those missiles off, you know.'

The Crystal Palace was totally silent, people watching the blank board for some sort of signal.

'No sign of activity,' Lem said, looking down at his readouts. 'Wait a second, sir. We're registering ...'

GREETINGS, PROFESSOR FALKEN.

'Why, hello, you bad boy,' Falken called out to the board, waving.

David typed in: HELLO.

A STRANGE GAME, Joshua said. THE ONLY WINNING MOVE IS NOT TO PLAY.

'And my boy Joshua likes to win!' Falken said quietly. He raised an inquisitive eyebrow at General Berringer. 'And you, sir. Do you like to win? Let's hope the Russians do.'

'Pardon me,' Berringer said, moving toward Colonel Conley. 'I've got a few calls to make.' He stopped by the colonel and turned around. 'Oh, and Falken. You know, you ought to consider resurrecting yourself.' Berringer turned a cold eye toward McKittrick. 'I have the feeling that at least one member of our personnel is going to need a little help sorting things out.'

On the screen flashed more words.

HOW ABOUT A NICE GAME OF CHESS, Joshua asked.

'Spot me your queen, and maybe!' McKittrick said, and Pat Healy almost collapsed into his arms, embracing him tightly.

'David, David, you're a genius, I love you!' Jennifer said, sitting in David's lap, arms around his neck, giving him a kiss.

'Hey, watch it. You might get Joshua jealous,' David said. 'And he's still got the launch codes.'

Jennifer laughed and boxed his ears playfully.

'Dr Falken,' David said, catching the man's attention. 'How good *is* Joshua at chess?'

'Oh, not very good, alas. Once a few Soviet masters played him, and beat him eight games out of ten.' Falken suddenly looked thoughtful. 'Goodness . . . I wonder . . .' he said, gazing up at the map of Russia. 'I would suppose those masters are back in their homeland by now . . .'

A frightened look flitted across the doctor's face.

Meanwhile, down on the otherwise jubilant floor, Radar Analyst Adler went to the first-aid cabinet to get a couple of much-needed Alka-Seltzer tablets.

All that was left were Extra-Strength Tylenol capsules.

Epilogue

Both computer rooms were empty this afternoon. Their doors were wide open. From his seat on the bench outside Vice-Principal Kessler's office, David Lightman could clearly see the list bearing the password that would allow him access to the Greater Seattle School Computer Network.

They'd given him his equipment back, somewhat worse for the experience of being taken apart and put back together, but otherwise in workable condition. What with all the confusion before and after this frightening business, he hadn't had any time to study. If he didn't do something drastic, he'd get wretched grades this quarter – and not just in biology.

It would be but the work of a moment to sneak in, take a peak at the six letters, and then scoot back to the bench.

David smiled to himself. How amusing! It wasn't even a temptation anymore! Not only was the challenge gone, but he honestly was simply not interested in changing his grades that way.

Besides, if he got caught crunching any more systems, the FBI had warned him ...

David Lightman shivered lightly at the thought, and dismissed it from his mind. No, better not to dwell on such things. He was lucky he and civilization were still around . . . and that he wasn't on the wrong side of a set of bars.

The highly varnished pine door opened. 'Kaiser' Kessler stuck his head through. 'Lightman?'

'Yes, sir?' David said, showing the new smile of respect he had for authority now.

'Lightman, good to see you.' Kessler gestured in a comradely fashion. 'C'mon in here, fellow.'

David followed the heavy-set man and sat down in the seat of honor. Kessler was already in his own chair, cleaning his glasses with a tissue.

'Well, now, Lightman. Your first day back, huh?'

'Yes, sir. There was what they call a debriefing. . . . I . . . uh . . . assume that you've been told everything?'

With a thick-fingered hand, Kessler opened a folder and studied a typed report for a moment. 'Yes. Those same agents who spoke to me originally about you paid a visit. They're quite impressed with you, Lightman, though not entirely in a positive fashion.'

'I'm sorry, sir.'

'Yes, I dare say you've had a bit of a traumatic experience, haven't you. How did it go with your parents?'

'They'll be okay.' David could not repress a slight smile. 'It's been quite a shock to them.'

'Do they know the whole story?'

'No sir, not the part about –' David caught himself.

'About almost getting blown to kingdom come?'

'You know about that, sir?'

Kessler nodded soberly. 'Yes, they thought it best to tell one person who could keep an eye on you . . . and although I suspect they would have liked to tell your parents as well, certain government personnel requested that the full story not be made known to them . . . for your sake.'

John McKittrick wasn't such a bad guy after all, David thought.

'No, David,' Kessler continued, 'only I know the whole story. It was necessary to get you back into school without me still thinking you were a traitor to the country. I must apologize. I said some nasty things about you to the FBI agents. But I'd like to think I know you better now. And I'd like to make amends.'

'That's really not necessary, sir. I think I've learned my lesson. My parents have been very good about it, sir. They're letting me keep my computer, and they're going to let me work at that summer job at NORAD that General Berringer got me.'

'I suppose you'll learn a great deal about computers there, won't you, David?'

'Yes, sir!' David Lightman said eagerly.

'Now then, in going over your case, I can see that some blame can be placed on our school system . . .' Kessler gave David a funny look, half suspicious, half awed. 'Three people called me personally concerning you in addition to the FBI agents – including Dr Stephen Falken. We had a long chat. I mean talk.'

'Oh.'

'Oh, indeed. We've been ignoring a great talent, David Lightman. This school has nothing much to offer the likes of you . . . and that's *our* fault. So, I'd like you to know that we are making radical changes in our curriculum to meet the needs of students like you.'

'You mean ... computer courses?' David was astonished.

'That's right.'

'Hands on?'

'I think we can afford a few Trash 80s or Commodores or Apples and Ataris.'

'Wonderful, sir. I'm sure that a lot of students will really enjoy it.'

'We'd like you to help out. We're thinking of starting a computer club. Interested in being our special advisor?'

'You *bet!*' David said.

'Terrific. Well now, I think that's about it, besides to say how astonished I am by this whole remarkable story.'

'It astonished me, too, sir.'

'One more thing,' Kessler said, standing up. 'I want to show you something. I want to show you that I'm not such a bad sort after all.'

Nonplussed, David followed the vice-principal out of the office, through the front door to the hallway.

Jennifer Mack registered surprise as they walked out together, Kessler's arm on David's shoulder in a fatherly fashion.

'Ah, Miss Mack,' said Kessler. 'Don't worry. I'm not going to take him to the Torture Chamber. Come on along. I want you to see this, too.'

Jennifer shrugged and followed, hugging her books to her chest.

Kessler took them to the school activities room. Since it was after normal school hours, the door to the room was closed. Kessler took out a key from a jangling chain and opened the door.

He turned on the light and pointed. 'Just over there, David. What do you think?'

In the corner, right by the Ping-Pong table and the water fountain, stood the familiar yet oddly out-of-place form of an arcade game.

'If this does well, I guess we can get a couple more, okay, David?'

David looked at the arcade game, astonished, and then looked at Jennifer. The light of amusement danced in her eyes. She stifled a laugh.

A Missile Command game!

'Now, David, I was playing with this thing a little earlier,' said Kessler, jingling through a pocket full of change. 'And I just can't get the hang of it.' He offered David some quarters. 'I wonder if you can show me a few tricks of the trade, so to speak.'

'Uh, no disrespect, sir!' David said, putting his arm around Jennifer and pulling her away, 'but I'm giving up arcade games for a while. Lent, you know.'

'Hey! Where are you going?' Kessler asked, astonished, watching as 'Mr Electric' himself walked away from his favorite computer game.

'We're going to be late for our aerobics class!' Jennifer called brightly over her shoulder. She leaned her head on David's shoulder as they walked toward the door.

On the way, David Lightman began whistling a certain Olivia Newton-John song he'd become quite attached to lately.